GEMMA

Gemma is a film star—a beautiful, sophisticated girl with clothes to match. So when she's sent to live with her Robinson cousins she's horrified. How *dull* to have to live with an ordinary family in an ordinary house.

But Gemma has a problem—she's terrified of attending the large comprehensive school. What will the other pupils think of a star who isn't being offered parts any more? Whatever happens, she mustn't be recognised, so she adopts her cousins' surname. But when it seems she's to stay for five years, she *has* to do something. She can't go on being a 'nobody'.

Gemma and Sisters, Gemma Alone and *Goodbye Gemma* are also Lions.

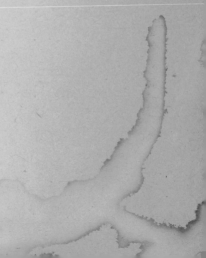

Gemima

Noel Streatfeild

Illustrated by Betty Maxey

COLLINS: LIONS

First published 1968
First published in Lions 1973
by William Collins Sons and Co Ltd
14 St James's Place, London S W 1
Third impression 1975

Printed in Great Britain
by Love and Malcomson Ltd,
Brighton Road, Redhill, Surrey

CONTENTS

CHAPTER ONE: EXTRAS

THE Robinsons lived in Headstone, an industrial town about 150 miles north of London. There were five of them: father, mother and three children. At the time this story begins Ann was eleven, Lydia—always called Lydie —was nine and Robin was seven. Robin had been christened Sebastian after Bach, but who would use a name like that, so he had settled for Robin as it was the first part of his surname.

Headstone, as a town, is proud of many things but of nothing so much as its orchestra. This is called "The Steen" and is world famous. The children's father, Philip Robinson, was a first violin in the orchestra and had dreamed of someday being its leader. Then he became ill with a form of rheumatism in his hands. This meant he had temporarily, it was hoped, to give up playing. The orchestra found him a job in their music library but it was a makeshift engagement for the orchestra already had a full-time librarian, so he earned far less than he had as a first violinist. This, of course, meant cuts in the Robinsons' style of living. The children's father, and their mother whose name was Alice, had a long talk on how they could best manage to economise without hurting anybody too much.

Alice was never a grumbler, somehow she managed to find something cheerful in the most depressing situations. It must have been a shattering blow, when you think your husband is in a good job until he retires, to watch it fold up under him. But if she was shattered there wasn't a sign of it.

"Well, as I always say, there's a brighter side to everything. Now, until your hands are right, at least I shan't have you going away for months on end on those overseas tours."

Philip had made some notes. He was a quiet man with the dedicated face so often seen on musicians.

"Thank goodness the house is ours. There are of course, the rates and so on, but there's no big out-going there."

They had been able to buy the house when they had married for Alice had inherited some money. It was just a red brick house in a rather ugly Victorian row, but they had looked after it well, and it had a garden. Anyway, to all the Robinsons it was "home", they never thought about whether it was ugly or not.

"I can cut down quite a bit on the housekeeping," Alice said. "It's easy really, I shall have to take a bit more trouble with my cooking to make things tasty. I'll see none of you notice the difference."

Philip looked at his notes.

"Robin will be eight in a few months. I thought I'd let him try for the choir school at the next entrance exam."

Headstone was hoping some day to build a cathedral. In the meantime there was St. Giles. This was a huge church which had been built and well endowed by one of the great industrial families at the end of the last century. St. Giles was something else of which Headstone was proud for it had a magnificent choir. The Robinsons had always hoped to send Robin to the choir school. It was a day school and gave a wonderful education. But it cost quite a lot so Alice knew, if Philip was talking of the choir school at that time, he was thinking of a scholarship. Her little Robin a St. Giles scholar!

"Do you think he has a chance?"

"I don't see why not. He has perfect pitch and he's a musical child."

"He doesn't sing half as well as Ann does."

Philip smiled.

"Ann's got a lovely voice but, alas, there are no choir

schools for girls, but I think Robin may develop a good voice when he's trained."

"I had hoped Ann could have singing lessons," Alice said.

"Some day she must. But I'm afraid for the time being all extras are out."

That made Alice catch her breath.

"Oh dear! Do you mean Lydie must give up her dancing lessons?"

"I'm afraid so. I gather that nine is quite young to start seriously, so if I am working again by next year it's still not too late for her to train if that is what she still wants."

Alice stifled a sigh.

"It'll be what she still wants. Is that all you have down on your list?"

"Just about. The others are personal things. I must keep out of the orchestra club room, it's surprising how much a round of beers adds up to. It's lucky I had already given up smoking. I've made a note too about the garden. We mustn't buy anything for it until my hands are right. But I'm sure we'll be given heaps of cuttings."

"Now it's my turn," Alice said. "I've got a part-time job."

Philip flushed. He hated to think of Alice working.

"Things aren't as bad as that."

Alice laughed.

"You sound as if I had said I was going shop-lifting. Actually I'm going to work in the Headstone General Hospital. It's to be on the switchboard and general dogsbody. Two to six daily. No Saturdays or Sundays and I have said I can't work during the school holidays. Couldn't fit better. I'm here to get lunch for you all and back in time to cook the supper. Ann will see to tea."

After that discussion Alice had talked things over with Ann. Ann was a sensible eleven-year-old. She was like her father with something of his dedicated look, but she had her fair straight hair from her mother, her father's hair was brown. She listened while her mother told her the

9

main economies they would make and about her job at the hospital. Then her mother said:

"The worst economy is extras. If Robin goes to St. Giles he will have to get a scholarship, and Lydie must give up her dancing classes."

Ann gasped when she heard about Lydia.

"Oh goodness! Poor Lydie! She'll hate that."

"I know, but if we are going to make a rule of no extras we can't make an exception for Lydie."

Ann thought about that.

"Robin and I don't want extras. Robin will get that scholarship if he wants to. You know how he is. If he doesn't get it that will only mean he doesn't want to go to St. Giles. I do wish there were choir schools for girls. So odd there aren't for lots of girls like me sing in choirs."

"I know, darling," her mother agreed, "that's what Dad and I were saying."

They were in the kitchen. Ann, who was a tidy child, straightened the plates drying in the plate rack.

"What's that thing Granny always says about penny wise?"

Her mother smiled. Philip's mother, who came every year to stay with them, was a great quoter of proverbs.

"Penny wise and pound foolish. It means people who are careful of pennies and careless with pounds. But that's not us. Lydie's dancing is pounds. Two pounds two shillings a term to be exact."

Ann knew what she wanted to say but it was hard to find the words.

"But wouldn't it be a kind of pound foolish if you stop paying for something now which could earn pounds and pounds in the end?"

Her mother thought about that.

"You may be right but I think it will be time enough for Lydie to learn when she's ten or even eleven, at least I hope so. Anyway, Dad has decided no extras so that's that."

And that was that.

10

Lydia's dancing teacher was told that at the end of that term Lydia would not, for the time being, be coming to dancing lessons. Robin's name was sent in to try for a scholarship at St. Giles. Ann hurried home from school every day to get tea for the family. And at Headstone General Hospital the matron said to her heads of staff: "I'm very sorry about poor Mr. Robinson's hands but what we did before we had Mrs. Robinson working for us I don't know. She's a jewel that woman."

What was not known to their parents was what the children felt about economies. Neither Lydia nor Robin said anything when their mother told them what was arranged, which surprised her for she was expecting an outcry from Lydia. But the reason why there was no outcry from her was because she knew she was not giving up her dancing classes.

Lydia was a pretty child. She had her mother's fair hair but she had a wave in hers. She had big blue eyes and was small for her age.

With her appearance and her smallness friends and her teachers at school were inclined to pet her. "'Lydie is such a darling."

This was true as long as Lydia got what she wanted, but she was anything but a darling if she did not get her own way over things that mattered to her. It was not often that this happened for what mattered to Lydia was to dance, and things to do with dancing. Mostly it was Ann and Robin who knew about this because quite often when Lydia refused to do things they were the only ones who knew why.

There were gym lessons at school. The term after Lydia had started learning to dance she had said to Ann:

"I shan't do that gym any more. It uses different bits of me to what I'm learning at my dancing."

"You'll have to do it," Ann had said. "We all have to."

Lydia had dismissed that.

"I shan't. I shall say 'My dancing teacher said I wasn't to'."

11

"Then they'll expect a letter from Mum about it," Ann had pointed out.

Lydia had practised a pirouette.

"They won't. You wait and see."

Lydia had been quite right. Looking innocent as an angel she had gone to the games' mistress.

"I can't do gym any more because my teacher says it's wrong for my dancing."

The gym mistress had smiled fondly down at her.

"All right, dear. Bring me a letter from your mother, will you?"

Lydia knew how to use her eyes. She had filled them with an expression of anxiety. At that time her father was still with the orchestra so that her mother was not working, but this did not worry Lydia.

"My Mum has to work. She doesn't get time to write letters and things like that any more."

The gym mistress had looked and felt sympathetic.

"All right, dear. You're excused gym and while we are doing it you can practise your dancing."

Then there was pocket money. When Philip had been a first violin pocket money had been a shilling a week to spend, but more had been forthcoming for extras, such as school charities and friends' birthday presents. The things Lydia wanted for her dancing could not be bought for a shilling and were certainly nothing to do with charities or birthdays. She wanted eau-de-Cologne and talcum powder for her feet, and nets and ribbon for her hair. None of these things were necessary, the beginners in her class did not use them, but Lydia had never considered herself a beginner; the big girls used eau-de-Cologne and talc powder and wore hair nets held in place by ribbon bands so she had to have those things too. Ann and Robin wondered she was not struck dead for the lies she told.

"Dad, could I have 2/6d for the United Nations?"

"Dad, could I have 2/- for Save the Children?"

"Dad, could I have 3/- for the life boats?"

If her father said, which he did sometimes:

"I can't think, Lydie, why you have to subscribe to so many charities in your class. Ann never seems to have so many."

Lydia would dismiss that with "Oh, if you don't want a life boat service", or whatever charity she had chosen. In those richer days she always got the money.

So after Lydia and Robin had heard about no extras neither Ann nor Robin were surprised when, as soon as they were alone, Lydia said:

"Dad can say what he likes about extras but I shall still learn dancing."

Ann felt worried for Lydia.

"It's not just the classes, there's shoes and things."

Lydia might have been a millionaire the way she spoke.

"They'll be bought."

Robin had accepted the news he was to try for a scholarship just as Ann had expected he would. It wouldn't happen until he was eight and that was months away. In the meantime there were much more interesting things happening. His father had taught them all simple theory of music and Robin had just discovered he could make up tunes and write them down. Who could fuss about a miles away scholarship who had discovered that?

"I expect I'll win one," he said casually. "I'll see how I feel about it when I'm eight."

Ann took no paying extras. She had persuaded her father and mother not to make her learn dancing.

"All I'll need is ballroom dancing, but not yet because the parties I go to don't do it."

But that did not say Ann was not ambitious. When Dad's hands had been well and he could play the piano he had taught her the beginnings of singing, but only the beginnings because he did not want her to strain her voice. Every night when she said her prayers she prayed "And please God let Dad's hands get well enough quite soon to play the piano just enough to teach me to sing."

"The children accepted that there could be no extras

13

quite calmly," the children's mother reported to their father.

Philip was proud of his family.

"Basically they are a sensible lot," he said.

CHAPTER TWO : LYDIA

LYDIA went to her next dancing lesson expecting Miss Arrowhead, whose school it was, to see her after her class. Miss Arrowhead herself did not teach Lydia, her niece Polly taught the beginners. Lydia had worked out that by her Saturday class Miss Arrowhead would have had her mother's letter explaining that she would not learn to dance next term. In her mind she had heard the conversation, Miss Arrowhead saying: "Oh, Polly, Lydia Robinson is not learning dancing after this term." She thought Polly would gasp and possibly scream "Lydia! That little genius! It's impossible, we must keep her even if we teach her for nothing." Anyway, however the conversation went, Miss Arrowhead would see her and say she would be proud to teach her for nothing. But after the Saturday class it was Polly who spoke to her and what she said was unbelievably unsatisfactory.

"Sorry you've got to give up coming to the classes for a bit. But don't worry, you'll just have to work extra hard when you can start again."

Lydia was furious. "Just have to work extra hard!" Couldn't that stupid Polly see that she was exceptional?

It was not Lydia's way to waste time when she wanted something. The big girls worked all Saturday morning with Miss Arrowhead coming to the studio as soon as the juniors' class finished. After her class Lydia changed her shoes and put on her coat and then sat down in a corner of the studio. Polly, hurrying out for she had a school class to take, saw her.

"What are you waiting for?"

"I'm going shopping with my Mum," Lydia said. "She's calling for me."

Polly nodded.

"You must be very quiet then or Miss Arrowhead will make you wait outside."

"How stupid grown-ups were," Lydia thought. "What sort of noise did Polly think she'd make sitting by herself?"

The big girls came in from the changing room. They wore white tunics and, in that class, pink belts. The belts changed colour as the pupils moved into more advanced classes. Lydia sighed with envy. How glorious to wear a white tunic with a pink belt!

The first half of the lesson the girls worked at the barre. It was not the first time Lydia had sneaked in to watch, so she knew that they would do grander versions of what in her class was just called "positions." She also knew that what these girls did on half pointes the much older girls did on their pointes. Lucky, lucky them!

Miss Arrowhead came in. She was a rather exciting-looking person, Lydia thought, sort of fierce. She had black hair and high cheekbones and a sharp nose. She was wearing a silk dress with a full skirt and soft shoes. She wasted no time.

"Demi-pliés," she said. "Twelve in all positions."

The pianist who played for all classes thumped out some chords. Demi-pliés were a slow half bend of the knees with the feet well turned out in each position. In her class Polly did not fuss about them too much but Miss Arrowhead was very particular.

"Place your weight correctly, girls. Winifred, you are allowing your feet to roll forward. Turn out those feet, Agnes. Think of your seat, Marion, it must be directly under you as your knees bend."

After the pliés the pupils worked at grand pliés, then

they came into the middle of the studio for Centre Practice. In Lydia's class there was nothing called Centre Practice, it was just called dancing. Lydia thought Centre Practice awfully dull for so much of it seemed to be arm exercises. But there was a little real dancing at the end. Then Miss Arrowhead clapped her hands.

"Thank you, girls. I will see you next Saturday. Meanwhile daily pliés please holding on to the towel rail or some suitable object. And, Agnes, keep those feet turned out and, Marion, please remember your seat."

Lydia had not thought Miss Arrowhead had seen her but she had for she came down the studio to speak to her.

"What are you doing here, child?"

To her Lydia told the truth.

"Waiting to speak to you."

"To me! Aren't you one of Polly's pupils?"

Lydia nodded.

"I'm Lydia Robinson. My Mum wrote you a letter."

Light dawned.

"Oh yes. You aren't going to learn for a term or two."

Lydia was shocked at the calm way Miss Arrowhead faced this fact.

"You can't talk like that. I must learn. I absolutely must. I'm going to be a very good dancer."

Miss Arrowhead looked amused.

"Are you now! Well, I've got five minutes, let's see what you can do. Change your shoes."

Lydia took off her coat and changed her shoes. In her class they wore ordinary frocks for their lessons. Knowing she was going to see Miss Arrowhead Lydia had put on her favourite, it was rose pink.

"What would you like me to do?"

"I'll see your pliés in all positions."

The pianist between classes went outside to have a cigarette so Lydia had to manage without music.

"I'll see six in each position."

Lydia hummed inside her head to keep time. She tried to remember all the things the class had been told. She

16

turned her toes out as far as they would go. She straightened her shoulders and her hips. She tucked her tail well in, she didn't want to be a Marion.

Lydia had got as far as the third position when Miss Arrowhead said:

"Take off your frock, child. I can't see your positioning with that stiff skirt."

Lydia scrambled out of her frock. She was wearing socks that day but her pants matched her frock so they would look all right. Then she came back to the barre.

After the pliés Miss Arrowhead told Lydia to go into the middle of the room and show her any steps she had learnt in Polly's class. Lydia, still humming music in her head, did jumps with foot changing, a pirouette or two and what Polly called cat jumps.

By now the next class had arrived; this did not worry Lydia for she liked an audience, but as well the pianist was back. Lydia looked at Miss Arrowhead.

"Mrs. Bennet's come back. Could she play the music for the Irish jig we learn?"

Miss Arrowhead turned to the girls of her next class.

"I won't keep you a minute. Sit, will you. The Irish jig please, Mrs. Bennet."

Lydia loved dancing the Irish jig, it was real dancing and not stopping all the time like exercises, and not babyish like skipping about pretending to be lambs. She was not a bit self-conscious though she was wearing only her vest and pants, her eyes shone and her body felt as if it was made of something as light as the seed of a dandelion. She had an audience of Miss Arrowhead and the big girls and she was dancing, truly dancing. The music stopped and she was back in the everyday world, just Lydia Robinson. Then something very unusual happened. The big girls clapped.

Miss Arrowhead smiled.

"Well done, Lydia. I will talk to Polly about you. See me after your class next Saturday."

To Lydia that was the longest week she had ever known.

17

What would Miss Arrowhead say? She must, she absolutely must do something for a child the big girls clapped.

The next Saturday Polly said:

"So you saw my aunt. Why didn't you tell me what you wanted? It was a lie that your mother was fetching you to shop, wasn't it?"

Lydia never thought things she had to make up to help her dancing were lies. Those were more like fairy stories, like "Cinderella" or "Red Riding Hood." Nobody said "This is a lie," before they told those stories.

"I don't think I know what a lie is," she explained. "It was just a story in case you wouldn't let me see her."

Polly laughed.

"You are a bad little thing. It will serve you right if my aunt beats you."

Miss Arrowhead came in at the end of the class. As soon as it was over she beckoned to Lydia.

"Come here, child. I have decided to grant you a scholarship. To begin with you will continue to learn with Polly but later, if you still show promise, I shall give you private lessons, and as well you will attend my class on Saturdays. I gather your father is for the moment unable to play his fiddle in The Steen. I greatly respect The Steen and that is why I'm glad to help you. I shall write to your parents about you."

Lydia was not sure that her father would not count things like dancing shoes as extras and so would say she couldn't take the scholarship. She was sure, if it was left to her, she would find a way to get everything she needed.

"Don't bother to write. I'll tell them."

Miss Arrowhead shook her head.

"No, thank you. I gather you told Polly a lie about why you waited after her class. That means I can't trust you."

Lydia for once felt ashamed.

"I'll never tell you a lie as long as I live. I absolutely promise I won't."

18

CHAPTER THREE: ROWENA

THE letter from Miss Arrowhead got a mixed reception.

"I'm very glad Lydia is thought worth a scholarship," Philip said to Alice, "and very nice of Miss Arrowhead saying it's partly because I played with The Steen, but in a way Lydia will be taking an extra. I mean, there's always something like shoes, and whatever it is they wear."

Alice was grateful for the scholarship for she was sure Lydia would have been very difficult next term if she had to stop learning.

"She's got shoes for the moment and they aren't expensive, and when she needs a tunic I can make it for her. It will be the same thing if Robin gets a scholarship. I know there will be a uniform grant for St. Giles choir school but I bet it won't cover everything."

"That means Ann will be the loser."

Alice laughed.

"What an old fusspot you are! I'll see Ann isn't the loser. When the next box of clothes comes from Rowena she shall have the pick, and I'll alter the clothes so they look like new."

Rowena was Alice's sister. They had been a family of four—herself, the eldest, then two boys and then Rowena. Their mother had died when Rowena was born so Alice, always the motherly type, had treated Rowena more like a little daughter than a younger sister. Without doubt between them they had spoilt Rowena, but even had her mother lived she would have been the odd one out. From a baby she had a vivid personality, she had to be the centre of every picture. She was an exceptionally amusing child and absolutely fearless. She had minded hurting those

19

whom she loved but she cared nothing about what outsiders thought; most of her school teachers found her unmanageable. Her father, Alice and her brothers had said laughingly that when Rowena grew up it was to be hoped there was an unmarried royal duke about for nothing less would suit Rowena.

Rowena had different plans. When she was sixteen, and was already very pretty, she had sent a photograph of herself to a newspaper which was running a beauty competition. She had won; her prize was money, clothes and a film test. It was no surprise to her family when, as a result of the film test, she received a good contract.

Aunt Rowena's story was the Robinson children's favourite. When they were small and one of them was ill they always refused to have books read to them, saying: "No, Mum, tell me about Aunt Rowena."

Actually, by the time the children were born, Aunt Rowena's film life was coming to an end. The sort of films that had made her famous were out of fashion and she was not right for the much starker films the public had taken to. But Aunt Rowena had never been one to accept ill-luck. If there was no work for her in films she must try something else. If she could not get work someone else must. The someone else was her daughter Gemma.

At one time in her career Aunt Rowena had married a film star called Basil Bow. The marriage had not lasted long for two film stars in one house did not make for harmony, so Basil had gone off and after they were divorced he had married someone else. Aunt Rowena was left with their daughter Gemma. Gemma had been a baby at the time her parents had separated and was looked after by a good Nannie. Alice had never seen Gemma, only her photographs—if it came to that she had not seen her sister Rowena for years, film stars didn't mix with a quiet housewife living in a back street in an industrial town. But the sisters remembered each other on birthdays and at Christmas and wrote to each other, Alice quite often, Rowena perhaps twice a year. But Rowena did see that all Gemma's cast-off clothes were sent to the Robinsons. Sometimes she enclosed a note saying: "If you can't use these pass them on to someone else"—or words to that effect. Thrifty Alice had never dreamt of passing on the clothes; they came from the best shops so she altered them for either Ann or Lydia.

Then Gemma began to become successful. She started off when she was four as a photographer's model. She was very photogenic, with some of her mother's prettiness but with a curious aloof, wistful charm that was entirely her own. It was no wonder she was spotted and soon was acting in films. By degrees she had become almost as famous as her mother. For the last six years there had been few good parts for children in films which she had not acted. In her films, some of which the Robinson children had seen, she was seldom well-dressed for her wistful charm made her perfect for the under-privileged types. She had been really magnificent as a child in an orphanage, and as a blind child she had sent every woman home from the cinema with their eyes swollen with tears. But when she was not acting Gemma was beautifully dressed. Everything in the latest fashion. Ann and Lydia were thrilled when a box of Gemma's clothes arrived, Gemma, though nearly the same age as Ann, was much smaller for her age, so most of her clothes with alterations could be let out to fit Ann or taken in to fit Lydia.

Now that Alice had mentioned Rowena Philip remembered something. He felt in his pocket and brought out his wallet.

"Someone left a paper in the music library. I happened to look at it and I saw this about your sister."

Alice took the piece he held out to her.

" 'I hear Rowena Alston is to star in a new TV serial,' " she read. " 'It's a lovely part,' she told me. 'Something quite new for me. I am really excited about it though a bit nervous, for, do you know, it's eight years since I made my last film.' "

"Goodness! " said Alice. "We must watch out for that

21

serial. It will be fun to see Rowena again. I wonder if she has changed much."

"Now I come to think of it we haven't seen Gemma in a film lately."

"Perhaps Rowena felt it was time she had an ordinary education. I read somewhere she had a good governess, but that's not the same thing as going to a school."

Philip smiled.

"You and your sister are a scream. I know you are devoted to her but all the news you get of her you read in the papers. I do wish something would bring her up this way."

"My goodness, I don't!" said Alice. "Imagine Rowena in our house meeting our friends. It would be like putting an osprey down in a chicken run."

"She could stay in an hotel and at least you could see her and have a good talk, instead of depending on newspaper gossip."

Alice thought back to the Rowena she had brought up.

"We don't need to have a talk. She knows where I am and how fond I am of her, and if she ever wanted me she'd say so. But we live in two worlds. I love mine and I suppose, odd though it seems, she loves hers. All the same I expect she likes to feel I'm here if she needs me."

"You're too unselfish," said Philip. "I suppose if Rowena were to call even now you'd run."

"I suppose I would," Alice agreed cheerfully. "After all, I brought her up. Somehow though I don't imagine she'll ever call."

But that was where Alice was wrong.

CHAPTER FOUR: THE LETTER

IT was in the spring that the letter came. Everybody was watching for the post for Robin had been to his voice trial for a scholarship for St. Giles choir school. Robin was the least interested in the post of the family for he was confident he had won his scholarship. But the moment there was the sound of a letter coming through the box Ann had jumped up from the dining-room table and run to fetch it. She came back looking disappointed.

"It isn't it. It's for you, Mum, it's typed."

Alice opened the letter.

"It's from Rowena," she said to Philip.

"Why does she use a typewriter?" Robin asked.

Alice smiled.

"She explains that in the first sentence. 'Excuse the typewriter but I'm at the studio all day so I have to dictate my letters. We have three more instalments of this serial to record.'"

The new serial had started on TV. It was exciting and much approved of by the Robinson children, who all thought Aunt Rowena was wonderful in it.

Alice read no more of the letter out loud. Instead, when she had finished reading it, she put it in the pocket of her cardigan.

"What's she say?" Lydia asked. "Is Gemma making a new film?"

Alice smiled.

"I've no time to tell you her news now. You ought to be getting ready for school and I've got a lot to do this morning."

Ann looked shrewdly at her mother.

"You're keeping something from us. You've got a sort of 'Don't look now' face, like you have when you're hiding something."

Alice laughed.

"If I have you won't hear until tonight so it's no good asking."

The children went different routes to school for Ann's Comprehensive was in one direction and Lydia's and Robin's Junior Mixed in the other. As Ann bicycled along she thought, as she often did, about Aunt Rowena and especially about Gemma. Gemma fascinated her. What could a girl who had led her sort of life be like? She pictured her driving everywhere in her own car with her own chauffeur. Probably, like royalty, she never travelled by bus and she would never have ridden a bike. She had heard an actress interviewed on TV who said that she rather liked making films because you felt so treasured. The reason, she had explained, was that the well-being of the actors was vital to the film, if they weren't happy the film might suffer. Ann tried to imagine a whole lot of people—film directors, camera crews, people who made you up and dressed you—caring all the time that you were happy. "I don't suppose," she thought as she turned the corner that led to her school, "I've ever had more than Dad and Mum caring if I'm happy. It must do something to you having everybody fuss over you."

Back at the house Alice was telling Philip what was in Rowena's letter.

"Some American film man has seen Rowena in her TV serial. He has offered her a part in a film over there. She is thrilled, it seems this could put her right back on the map. But she doesn't want to take Gemma to America. She says she is at the awkward age and she wouldn't be able to look after her so . . ."

Philip interrupted.

"So will we have her."

"Yes. She will pay quite a lot so it would be a help just now. Anyway I don't see how we can refuse."

"And anyway," said Philip, "you wouldn't want to say no."

Alice considered that.

"I couldn't very well, she is my niece."

"And you've always wanted to see her."

"That's true," Alice agreed.

Philip spoke seriously.

"You know you once said having Rowena here would be like putting down an osprey in a chicken run. Are you sure Gemma won't be an osprey?"

Alice laughed.

"Not for long. She's a child, she's two months younger than Ann. I'm sure living with us she'll soon be just a normal girl."

Philip saw it was no use arguing, and he knew it was right that they should take Gemma, and, of course, the money would be useful, but he felt Alice ought to look the facts clearly in the face.

"I wonder what the children will say, particularly Ann for Gemma will go to her school."

"I should think they would be thrilled, they've always wished they could meet her."

"Meeting people is very different from having them to live with you."

Alice made a face at him.

"It's time you were off to the music library."

Philip got up.

"Will you give up working in the hospital?"

Alice shook her head.

"I doubt it. I love it. But I might cut down my hours a bit. The mornings are a shocking rush and today will be worse than usual as I must write to Rowena."

That evening over supper Alice told the children the news.

"Your Aunt Rowena is to make a film in Hollywood. While she's making it Gemma is coming to live with us."

If she had said that the Queen was coming to tea the children would not have been more startled.

25

"Gemma coming here!" said Lydia. "I should think you'll have to paint the house and have new curtains."

"Won't she be awfully grand?" Robin asked. "We don't want anybody being grand in this house."

Ann looked worried.

"Where's she to sleep? If she's in the spare-room Gran can never come to stay."

The house had four bedrooms: The parents' room, the room shared by Ann and Lydia and a little room which was Robin's and a spare-room. Philip's mother, the children's Gran, was a widow, she had five children and, though she had a home of her own, spent a large portion of each year visiting them in turn. She usually spent six weeks with her son Philip.

"And it's not only Gran," Lydia pointed out. "If Gemma's in the spare-room where's Grandad to stay?"

Grandad was Alice's father. Her two brothers had emigrated to Canada and their father lived with one of them. But two years before he had been over on a visit and had stayed with the Robinsons. The visit had been an enormous success and he had promised some day to repeat it.

"Grandad isn't coming this year," said Alice, "but I have been thinking about Gran. I was wondering if I could turn the boxroom into a bedroom for Gemma. I read a wonderful advertisement somewhere which said: 'Why not turn that boxroom into a cosy bedroom-study?'"

Ann thought if there was going to be a bedroom-study she would like to have it. But before she could speak Lydia burst out:

"Oh please, Mum, could I have it? You could have a barre fixed so I could practise my dancing. And Gemma would like sharing with Ann, they're the same age."

"I haven't decided anything," Alice said firmly, "not even to turn the boxroom into a bedroom. If I do we'll have to talk over who shall have it. I had thought of it for Gemma but family come first, and that means if you want it, Ann, you shall have it."

"That's not fair," Lydia protested. "I don't want to share with Gemma."

"It seems to me, Lydie," her father said, "that you were suggesting Ann should share with her; what's sauce for the goose is sauce for the gander as your Gran would say."

"When's she coming, Mum?" Robin asked.

"I wrote we'd love to have her the moment she's ready to come, which will be quite soon I think."

Ann caught her breath. Gemma coming soon! Wouldn't she spoil things with her grand ideas? Out loud she said:

"We are so happy as we are being just us."

Philip gave her a sympathetic look but his voice was stern.

"And we shall be just as happy with Gemma here. If, as a family, we are worth anything we won't be put off our stroke because there's an extra child in the house."

"Not us," Lydia agreed. "She can huff and puff as much as she likes but she won't blow our house in."

They all laughed at that but Alice felt worried. Surely, she thought, poor little Gemma ought not to be compared with the big bad wolf.

CHAPTER FIVE: GEMMA

A MONTH later Gemma arrived. It was the beginning of the Easter holidays so all the family were on the platform to meet her except Philip, who could not get time off from his music library.

Having seen her on films the children supposed they would recognise her at once, but the Gemma who arrived didn't look as they expected her to look. As a result they missed her, and when they found her she had already collected a porter who was piling her heap of smart luggage on to a trolley.

"Gemma dear, there you are! " said Alice, kissing her. "I'm sorry we missed you but we were looking at the wrong end of the train."

Robin stared at Gemma, who looked smarter than any girl he had ever met.

"Actually we didn't know you would be in a first-class carriage, we were looking in second-class."

Lydia was quite dazzled by Gemma in the flesh. She was dressed in a vivid shade of yellow against which her long fair hair looked almost white.

"We didn't know you had fair hair, at least not as fair as that. It looked brown when you were in that orphanage film."

Ann, with a sinking heart, saw Gemma look at each of them in turn with eyes like flints. How could she know that Gemma's eyes were hard because she was unhappy and scared and trying not to cry? Or how could she know that stage-trained Gemma had thought a lot about her first meeting with the strange cousins? She had planned her entrance, hoping to have a porter and all her luggage piled up before they saw her. "I'm a film star," she told herself, "and the first time they see me I've got to look like one."

As Gemma had so much luggage Alice told the children to walk home, she would ride with Gemma in a taxi.

"Do you know," said Robin when the taxi had driven off, "Gemma gave that porter five whole shillings."

"Showing off," said Lydia. "I'm glad you're sharing a room with her, Ann, and not me."

The question of whether Gemma should sleep in the newly-decorated boxroom had settled itself. It was in the roof and so had a sloping ceiling, which made it impossible to find room for a cupboard. There was an arrangement with curtains for hanging clothes, but Alice felt it was unsuitable for Gemma's probably vast wardrobe. She had talked the matter over with Ann.

"You can have the little room if you want to, darling, but I wish you would share with Gemma. She's just your age."

Ann would have loved to have a room to herself but if anyone was to share with Gemma she could see she was more suitable than Lydia. So she had agreed. But that did not mean she wanted Lydia swanking because she had won the boxroom.

"I bet Gemma doesn't show off any more than you do. Look at the way you danced at the station."

"And stood on one leg holding the other up in the air so everybody stared," said Robin.

"That's not showing off," Lydia retorted. "It's practising. Anyway if I show off it's better I have my own room. Imagine two people showing off at once."

In the taxi Alice was struggling to get to know Gemma. She took her hand and gave it a squeeze.

"It is such fun having you with us, you can't think how I've always longed to know you. You see, I brought up your mother."

Gemma did not return the squeeze, in fact to Alice Gemma's hand lying in hers felt as unresponsive as if it was a stuffed glove. When Gemma answered it was in a remote, chilly voice.

"Yes, I know you did. Mummy has often told me."

"Which day does she leave?"

Gemma swallowed. Why must Aunt Alice talk about Mummy? Why must she talk at all? Couldn't she see she wanted to be left alone?

"Tomorrow."

"So exciting for her," said Alice. "I'm sure she must have missed making films."

Gemma could think of no answer to that. "Missed" was an idiotic word for what Mummy had felt. Why, sometimes she had been so frustrated she had howled like a dog. However, aunts, however silly, must be answered.

"Oh yes, she did."

Alice, later telling Philip about the drive, said: "You

never saw anyone look such a fool as me. I was like a gauche schoolgirl, I wanted to leave go of Gemma's hand but I didn't know how to." By then she could laugh at herself but she was anything but laughing in the taxi. She racked her brain for something to say.

"You're sharing a bedroom with Ann. I hope you don't mind sharing."

Gemma was appalled. It was bad enough having to stay with the cousins in this hideous town. But sharing a room was worse than anything she had thought of. She pulled her hand away from Alice's and made no attempt to sound polite.

"How should I know if I mind? I've never been asked to share before."

Alice stopped feeling like a gauche schoolgirl and instead was angry. No spoilt chit was going to talk to her like that.

"Sharing a room won't be the only thing that is strange to you. Ours is just an ordinary little house, and we live very ordinary lives and have very ordinary friends."

Gemma was sunk in such gloom that she didn't care if she had offended her aunt. She shrugged herself down inside her yellow coat and, in case her hand should be taken again, thrust both into her pockets.

Alice looked at Gemma out of the corners of her eyes. Oh dear, why had she lost her temper? Poor little Gemma, she was probably feeling strange and homesick and hating her mother going away. But it was no good saying anything to a child who clearly was asking to be let alone. In silence they drove the rest of the journey until they turned into the street where they lived.

"This is Trelawny Drive, we are the last house but one on the left."

Gemma, through glazed eyes, looked at Trelawny Drive. Mummy laughingly had said: "I can't imagine what Trelawny Drive is like. Rather like that street they used in those shots of the orphanage in your last picture I imagine." And Mummy had imagined right. Trelawny

Drive was painfully like the dreary street used in the film.

"Fancy!" she said and then, trying to find more, she added: "Aren't the houses like each other."

Gemma's luggage was in the hall when the children got home. Their mother came to the door to meet them. She had got a grip on herself and not by a flicker of an eyelash did she show what a gloomy view she took of her niece.

"Tea's ready. Gemma's tidying. After tea would you all help with the luggage. I don't want Dad to see it or he'll insist on carrying it up, which will be bad for his hands."

Tea passed off better than Alice had dreamed that it could.

"I suppose you've been watching Aunt Rowena's serial?" Lydia asked Gemma.

Gemma was glad of a subject which distracted her from what seemed to her a dreadfully depressing little house. Used to a big luxury flat she felt shut in and cramped.

"Of course. Mummy and I have been watching it together."

"Isn't it odd seeing yourself, I mean for Aunt Rowena?" Robin asked.

Gemma was at once the knowledgeable actress.

"You get used to it, and, of course, you learn. I mean there's nothing like watching yourself to see what you've done wrong."

Ann helped herself to some jam.

"We don't think Aunt Rowena does anything wrong. We think she's marvellous."

Robin bounced on his chair in his eagerness to get heard.

"What happens next? Does that man get all her money?"

"Don't tell him, Gemma," said Alice. "It's the Friday night treat seeing the serial."

"We are allowed to sit up for it," Lydia explained.

"Even Dad likes it," Ann said. "And he hardly ever watches television."

Alice laughed.

"Poor man, he has to watch the serial whether he likes it or not for on Fridays, while it lasts, we have supper in front of the TV set."

"We call it Telly-supper," Lydia explained. "It's things to eat in your fingers."

"Have some more bread, Gemma," Alice said, "or would you like a bun?"

Gemma started. When she had sat down she had known she couldn't swallow a thing. She wasn't hungry and there was a lump in her throat. But somehow, with everybody talking at once, and being interested in the serial, she had eaten a whole slice of bread spread with butter and strawberry jam and she had liked it. However awful some things were perhaps it wouldn't be too bad being part of a family.

"I'd like a bun, please."

Almost she smiled, thought Alice. "Oh dear, I do hope it means she isn't going to be too difficult."

CHAPTER SIX: THE BEDROOM

THAT evening Ann had to go out. She sang in her church choir and it was choir practice night, so she was not there when Gemma unpacked. Alice, rather apologetically, had shown Gemma what cupboard space she could have and where she could put her personal possessions.

"I do hope you'll have room, dear, if not perhaps we could get a larger cupboard. You'll see that half of the chest of drawers' top and half the mantelpiece are empty, that is for your things. When your cases are empty put them outside. We are using a shed in the garden for luggage as we've turned the boxroom into an extra bedroom."

32

With all the rush of her mother's shopping and packing, and her own packing, Gemma had not had time to picture her life with the cousins. Now, left alone to unpack, a wave of desolation swept over her. She had never realised how used she was to pretty things around her. Her bedroom in the London flat was white and green, everything beautifully made to match. This room seemed to her all odds and ends and hideous. There was a huge mahogany wardrobe, there was a big shining yellowish chest of drawers. The curtains and the two bedspreads matched but they were a darkish blue, more useful than pretty.

Gemma drearily examined Ann's possessions on the chest of drawers and on the mantelpiece. There was a little bust of Mozart; Gemma knew whose bust it was because the name was written in the clay. There was a collection of books held up with book-ends, they were not Gemma's sort of books because they were all about music. There was a bookshelf under the window which looked more promising, but none of the books were very new and she felt sure she would find she had read most of them. Ann seemed to collect glass animals for there were a lot of them on her half of the mantelpiece, and she seemed fond of stones for there were several about which looked as if they had been picked up off a beach. Over the dressing-table there was a big photograph of what must be The Steen orchestra for Uncle Philip was there playing the violin. On the mantelpiece there was a frame holding snapshots of the family, apparently on holiday. Altogether Gemma decided Ann had very shoddy-looking possessions.

Gemma was bitterly hurt. All her life she had known she and Mummy were everything to each other. It had, therefore, been a cruel shock when her mother had told her that she was off to America leaving her behind at Headstone. Gemma, unable to believe her mother would leave her, had implored to go to America too, but she had been put off with evasive answers, until suddenly her mother had decided on plain speaking.

"You'd be in the way, Gemma. You're not a little girl any more to be sent off with a Nannie. I couldn't look after you."

Gemma, when hurt, longed to hurt back. She had not been able to hurt her mother, who was full of excitement at the thought of being back in pictures. But the wanting to hurt remained and now she could take it out on Ann. She tore open the case in which she had packed her personal possessions. Carefully wrapped in tissue paper were several framed photographs of her mother and of herself in various films. There was her chiming silver clock. There were two beautiful boxes in flame-coloured silk, one for handkerchiefs and the other for her jewellery. There were ten exquisite pieces of Copenhagen china. Then she unpacked her dressing-table set. Blue enamel and silver with her initials on each piece. She placed then carefully on her side of the dressing-table. "That'll show you the sort of things I'm used to," she thought as she looked at Ann's simple brush and comb.

Yet when everything was unpacked and squeezed into the available space it wasn't pride Gemma felt but just misery. When she had said she was going up to unpack Aunt Alice had said: "Then I expect you'll be glad to go to bed. You've had a long day and Ann generally goes straight up after choir practice." Gemma had kissed her aunt and uncle saying "Good-night" but at the time she had wondered if she would want to go to bed so early. But now, the unpacking finished and the cases stacked outside the door, she found she was thankful she had not to go downstairs again. She had managed all day not to cry but now she knew she had to. Everything was so awful. This incredibly dreary house. Living here would be so intolerably dull. There was the terrifying school to face. It was too much. In bed Gemma rolled over on to her face and sobbed and sobbed.

Gemma was crying so hard that she did not hear Ann

open the door, and she only knew she was in the room when the light was turned on.

Ann heard Gemma crying and forgetting she was the grand cousin, only knowing she was unhappy just as she would be if separated from her mother, she ran to Gemma's bed and put an arm round her.

"Don't cry, Gemma. I know it's hateful for you being left with us while your mother is in America. We are all awfully sorry for you."

That was Gemma's worst blow. The cousins sorry for her! She, Gemma Bow, who had meant to stun them with her glory! All the bitterness in her heart poured out. She sat up, her eyes blazing.

"Nobody need be sorry for me. Look at all I've got. Why, my things make your things look silly. What I'm crying about is having to live in this miserable slummy little house. You should see our flat in London, it's perfect. I hate everything here."

Ann was a mild child as a rule, but there were things nobody could take. Her home called a miserable slummy little house! She lifted her hand and gave Gemma a really hard slap on the cheek.

The blow startled them both. Ann because she had not known she could hit anybody, and Gemma because she had not imagined anyone would dare hit her. The two girls gazed at each other in shocked surprise.

"I say, I am sorry," said Ann. "I shouldn't have hit you. It was beastly of me. But you shouldn't have said this house was slummy."

Gemma knew this was true, it was hateful of her. She held her cheek, which was stinging. But oddly she felt better.

"No, I shouldn't have. I only said it because I'm miserable about other things."

Ann got up and walked round the room looking at Gemma's belongings.

"I don't suppose you feel like talking to me, I mean after I've hit you, but if it's any good you could tell me

35

how miserable you feel. I wouldn't tell anybody else, not even Mum, unless you said I could."

Gemma watched Ann pick up a Copenhagen china faun.

"I collect Copenhagen. Mummy gave me that faun last Christmas. It was in my stocking."

Ann put down the faun and came back to the bed.

"We know it's not a bit like you are used to here, but we have fun. Wasn't it a bit dull working alone with a governess?"

Gemma had nothing with which to compare working with a governess.

"I don't think so. When I wasn't making a picture, like this last year, my governess often took me to places where history happened, like the Tower of London and Hampton Court."

"Lucky you," said Ann. "Did you like your governess?"

Gemma thought rather contemptuously of poor Miss Court. So proud of her film star pupil. So sure she must be a wonderfully clever child, off the film set as well as on it.

"She was all right, I suppose." Then she grinned. "Actually she was a bit of a fool."

"I can't imagine a governess. I've only known schools. I wonder how you'll like going to the Comprehensive. I found it queer at first, it's so big." Then she stopped. "What's the matter? You look awfully queer."

Gemma was clutching her solar plexus.

"Don't tell me about the school. It hurts me here. Not to-night but sometime I'll try and explain. Please, Ann, talk about something else."

Ann began to undress, wondering what on earth was worrying this strange cousin.

"O.K. I'll tell you about Lydie and her dancing school." Then, feeling rather awkward, she said: "I vote we don't tell anyone about to-night what you said, and that I hit you."

36

Gemma agreed at once.
"Don't let's. Go on about Lydie."

CHAPTER SEVEN: SCHOOL UNIFORM

WHATEVER else Gemma had expected to find when she came to Headstone it was not talented cousins. Everybody, including her mother, had suggested that it would be exciting for the Robinsons to have her to live with them. Miss Court had been certain of it.

"I expect they're making great preparations for your arrival, dear," she had said. "They won't be used to meeting people like you."

"I'd take lots of your film stills," her mother had suggested. "Those sort of things are sure to thrill your cousins."

"I just can't see Gemma in a place like Headstone," friends had cackled. "You'll certainly shake them up a bit, Gemma darling."

But Gemma, struggling to get used to the house and the ways of the household, found that far from being shaken up by her arrival the cousins each had their own life and refused to be impressed by hers. Not that they did not accept that she had lived a totally different life from theirs, and would therefore be unused to the ordinary everyday things, they did.

"Robin and me are going shopping for Mum," Lydia told her. "Would you like to come? I don't suppose you've ever been in a self-service store, have you?"

During the last year when lessons were finished and Miss Court had gone home Gemma had often been at a loose end, and had been only too glad to go shopping with the daily housekeeper, and much of the shopping had been in a self-service store. But if Lydia and Robin supposed no film star had ever been in one she was willing to agree.

"I'd love to come. Tell me what we do."

"We all take turns with helping in the house," Ann told her, "but I don't suppose you've ever done anything like that, have you, so Mum said you could come to it gradually."

Gemma never had done anything like that. Her mother was hopelessly undomesticated and had brought her daughter up the same way—to leave everything to the daily staff. Gemma would not have minded learning, but if the cousins thought she was too grand for that sort of thing then she would agree with them.

What Gemma found it impossible to understand was that you could have talent and just accept it and say nothing about it. In her world, in theatre dressing-rooms and on the telephone, there were cries of "Darling, you were wonderful!" "Gemma sweet, you really are a talented child. You made me cry my poor eyes out in your last picture." "Rowena angel, that serial would be nothing without you, and you look divine." But here nobody talked about what you did. She had been in the house three days when the letter arrived saying Robin had won a scholarship to the choir school.

"You better make the best of this holiday, Robin," his father said, "for next Easter you will be very busy."

"I shan't mind," said Robin, "and I'll be busy at Christmas."

His mother had been looking through a printed book which came with the news of the scholarship.

"They give piano lessons. That'll be a help until your hands are well, Philip."

"Good! " said Robin. "I was hoping they'd teach that."

Gemma tried to understand.

"Was it a difficult scholarship to get?"

Ann nodded.

"There were only three vacancies and heaps of boys tried for them."

38

Her uncle turned to Gemma.

"St. Giles is a very good school and only part of it is the choir school. Each year a few scholarships are offered for choristers, and, of course, there are plenty of applicants because it's a way of getting into the school which, if you have to pay, isn't cheap."

Gemma looked at Robin with respect.

"You must sing very well. I didn't know."

Robin dismissed that.

"I don't—not yet."

"He's musical and has a good ear," said his father. "He'll learn."

Then there was Lydia. Ann had told her Lydia had a scholarship at the dancing school. Gemma had imagined Lydia skipping about as a butterfly or a lamb, but one day she was taken by Alice to pick Lydia up after her Saturday morning class. By that Easter Lydia was being taught by Miss Arrowhead. Gemma and her aunt waited outside the studio but through the window Gemma could see Lydia in a white tunic with a pink belt, her hair held off her neck in a net, standing in a row with the rest of her class. Miss Arrowhead was showing them a series of steps. When she had finished each of the girls danced the enchaînement by themselves. Some badly, some reasonably well. Then it was Lydia's turn and there was no doubt about it, she was good. Gemma turned to her aunt.

"But Lydie's marvellous!"

Alice had not been looking.

"Oh no, dear, not marvellous. You mustn't put ideas into her head but I believe she's coming on nicely."

Perhaps the biggest surprise of all was Ann. Quiet, friendly Ann whom Gemma had come to think of as the untalented one of the family. They were in the bedroom and Gemma was hanging something up when she saw a frock Ann had inherited from her. It was white and silver and had been specially designed for her to wear at the first night of one of her films. "I don't think it's any good our sending this to my sister," her mother had said to

Miss Court. "When could a child wear it in a place like Headstone?" "Where shall I send it then?" Miss Court had asked. Rowena, who was in a turning-out mood, "Oh, send it with the rest. They can sell it if they can't use it." Now Gemma took the frock out of the cupboard.

"I remember this. Have you ever worn it?"

Ann took the frock from her and hugged it to her.

"Lots and lots of times. It's my concert dress. Mum says it's getting skimpy on me but I love it so much I'll hate to give it up."

"Your concert dress?" said Gemma. "What concerts?"

"I sing at them," Ann explained. "Always at church concerts because I'm the choir soloist, and sometimes for old people and things like that."

"I never knew you sang, I mean by yourself. What sort of songs?"

"All sorts," said Ann casually as she put the dress back in the cupboard. "At Christmas there were six concerts."

Gemma was amazed.

"And people write and ask you?"

"No, mostly they write to Dad. He fixes the programmes for me."

"I see," said Gemma, but she didn't see at all. One cousin who sang at concerts. One who could dance and one who could win a scholarship at a choir school, and never a hint in all those letters that Aunt Alice had written that her children were good at anything.

It was a week before the end of the holidays when Alice said at breakfast:

"We must go shopping today, Gemma. I must get you your school uniform."

"It's simply awful," Lydia told her. "Grey skirts with purple blazers and a purple hat."

"She won't have the purple hat, Lydie," Ann pointed out. "In the summer it's straw with a purple band."

"And you wear a white blouse with a purple tie," Lydia went on, "and nobody looks nice in any of it. I simply dread the day when I'm old enough to go there."

"I wonder if you and Ann will be in the same class," said Philip.

Ann shook her head.

"Oh no, she'll be above me. After all, she's had a governess teaching only her."

Alice turned smiling to Gemma. Then the smile froze.

"Gemma child, what's the matter? You look as white as a sheet."

"It's nothing—nothing really," Gemma whispered. "It's just I don't feel very well."

Alice got up and helped Gemma out of her chair.

"Come on, chickabiddy. Bed is the best place for you."

"That was odd," said Lydia. "She looked all right when she came down."

"I looked all right the day after Christmas and suddenly I was sick as sick," Robin remarked. "Do you remember?"

Ann shuddered.

"I should think we do. It was disgusting," but her mind was on Gemma. What was it she had said the night she arrived? "Don't tell me about the school. It hurts me here. Not tonight but some day I'll try and explain." Now, when her mother had talked about buying her school uniform, Gemma had nearly fainted. "Poor Gemma," she thought. "As soon as Mum's out of the way I'll talk to her and try to find out what's up."

CHAPTER EIGHT: GEMMA TELLS

In bed with a hot water bottle Gemma soon felt better, but she still looked shaken and peaky.

"Oh good!" Alice said when Ann came in. "Here's company for you. You stay with Gemma, Ann, I'll manage without you this morning."

41

When the girls were alone Ann sat down on Gemma's bed.

"It was because Mum said she had to buy your uniform that you felt ill, wasn't it?"

Gemma was clutching the hot water bottle to her solar plexus. Now she gripped it even tighter and fixed her scared blue eyes on Ann.

"Don't ask. Don't talk about it or I'll be sick."

Ann, in the two weeks Gemma had been in the house, had learnt that she exaggerated. Things were never just nice or nasty to her, they were terrific or ghastly or shattering. So she was not put off by threats of being sick. Gemma would have to have school uniform, just as she would have to go to school, so she might as well face up to it.

"You better tell me what you're fussing about. I mean, whatever it makes you feel you'll have to go to school. If I knew what was up I might help."

Gemma writhed as if she was in pain.

"Nobody can help. It's inside me." She choked and tears ran down her cheeks.

Ann hated to hurt Gemma when she was so down, but she must if she was to help.

"Come on. Crying won't help. Our Gran—that's Dad's Mum who comes to stay every year—always quotes proverbs and one of them she's specially fond of is 'Troubles shared are troubles halved.' It could be true. Try it and see."

Gemma thought this over. Even thinking of explaining everything to Ann made her feel a shade better. The worries coiled up in her inside like overwound springs relaxed slightly.

"If I tell you you won't tell the others. Lydie would laugh, I know she would."

"Of course I won't tell anybody if you don't want me to."

Gemma licked her lips, trying to guess where she should begin.

"I know you all think I'm a grand film star. Well, I am in a way." Gemma stopped. "No, I'm not going to lie to you, I'll tell you everything. I was starring in films but I'm at the wrong age now. My agents haven't had any offers for me for over a year. I'm washed up."

Ann nodded.

"We know you haven't acted in a picture for ages but I expect another will turn up."

Gemma shook her head.

"Not a film, when I'm twelve I might get some TV work, but I'm only just eleven."

"Why when you're twelve?"

Gemma was surprised Ann didn't know.

"I can have a licence then. You can't appear live before an audience until you have a licence."

"But you can be on films?" Ann was puzzled. "That sounds silly to me."

"It's the law," said Gemma. "You can't argue with the law."

Ann could not see what all this had to do with going to school.

"Is it you don't want to be in school when you're twelve?"

"No." Gemma sat up. "It's that I'm scared of going to school. You must see, Ann, how awful it is for me. They'll mostly know my name at school, many of them will have seen my pictures. Can't you hear them wondering what a film star is doing in a school in Headstone! They'll see I'm washed up and they'll be sorry for me, I know they will and that is something I simply couldn't bear."

Ann thought this over. She had only been to the Comprehensive since last autumn and she still felt a new girl. The school was so enormous, there were a thousand pupils, it was easy to feel insignificant. But, somehow, news got around for last term she had been tested and accepted for the school choir. There was no doubt about it, most of the girls, and probably the boys too, would know Gemma by name and many of them would have seen her pictures. It probably would be a bit of a sensation when she turned up at Headstone Comprehensive. She could almost hear and see the nudges and the whispers. And probably Gemma was right, it would be thought a bit of a come-down for a film star.

Ann was painfully conscious she didn't believe what she was saying, and that she sounded like it.

"They'll soon get used to you being there."

"But that's not all," Gemma went on. "Miss Court was quite a good governess I suppose, but lots of the time I wouldn't learn and she wouldn't make me. Well, she sort of admired me when I was acting and thought it was a privilege to teach me, she often said so."

"A privilege!" gasped Ann, stunned by such a vision. "Imagine anyone saying that! I think I'd drop dead if anyone said it to me."

Gemma, now started on her story, was not put off by interruptions.

"Of course, whether you are a child actress or a child skater or anything like that you have to do five hours lessons a day. Usually I did my lessons in the morning and filmed in the afternoon, but sometimes it didn't work out like that and Miss Court had to squeeze my lesson time in, well, I didn't always feel like lessons—well, would you when you were working on the set all day? Anyway, what I'm getting at is I'm almost sure I'm very, very backward."

Ann could not see why that mattered.

"You'll catch up."

"That's not the point," said Gemma. "How would you like to appear in a huge school as a very backward washed-up film star? Me! Everyone's always admired me and said I was clever. Oh, I shall feel so miserable and so ashamed!" Gemma flung herself back on her pillows and howled. Between her sobs she gasped: "I never stop thinking about it, I'm so worried it hurts all the time."

Ann looked at Gemma's heaving shoulders. "Poor Gemma," she thought. "I suppose I do sort of understand
44

how she feels. It will be pretty ghastly for her after being so important. But what can I do to help?" Then she had an idea. She laid one hand on Gemma's heaving shoulders.

"Gemma, stop howling for a minute and listen. Let me tell Mum. She's full of good ideas, perhaps she'll think of a way to help. She might let you have another governess or something. Anyway, let me tell her. She wouldn't want you to be miserable like this."

Gemma, through her sobs, heard what Ann said. Could Aunt Alice help? Could Aunt Alice find Miss Court or someone like her? If she could she would work and work, she would promise that. She would promise anything if only she need not go to a school where they would point her out and whisper pityingly about her.

"All right. Tell Aunt Alice, but not Lydie or Robin."

"Leave it to me," said Ann.

It was easy for Ann to talk to her mother alone for she had sent Lydia and Robin out to do the shopping. She was in the kitchen mincing meat for a cottage pie.

"Hullo, darling," she said. "How's Gemma now?"

Ann sprawled across the kitchen table while she poured out what Gemma had told her.

"I sort of see what she means," she finished up. "It's perfectly true, everybody will think it odd, a big star like Gemma being at Headstone Comprehensive, and some of them will say she's washed-up."

Alice went on mincing the meat. She was evidently thinking for she did not answer at once. Then she said:

"I detest the expression 'washed-up' but I suppose the truth is that for the time being that is what has happened to Gemma."

"Imagine it happening when you are eleven," said Ann. "Why, we're only just beginning to do things."

"That's as it should be. It's bad luck on poor Gemma that she was a success so young, and even more bad luck that her mother doesn't seem to have brought her up very sensibly."

"Couldn't you do something?" Ann urged. "She really is terribly unhappy."

Alice had finished mincing. She tipped the meat into a bowl and began cutting up onions to mix with it.

"What sort of something? She has to go to school you know, it's the law of the land."

"Couldn't she have another governess?"

"From what Gemma says a governess hasn't been a great success. Besides, it will do her good to go to school. She hasn't mixed enough on ordinary terms with other children."

Ann put a finger into the mashed potato which was waiting to cover the cottage pie and ate what she collected.

"It's no good talking like someone on a TV broadcast. She's truly dreadfully unhappy. I knew there was something worrying her the day she arrived."

"There'll be something worrying you, Ann Robinson," said her mother, moving the potato bowl, "if you eat my potato." Then she straightened up and stared at Ann. "I believe I've got a solution. It came to me as I was speaking."

"What?"

Alice cleaned her hands on a cloth.

"Gemma must hear first. I think it's a good idea but she may not agree."

Gemma had reached that state when you don't want to cry any more but you can't stop yourself.

Alice went to the basin and soaked a face flannel in cold water. She brought it to the bed.

"Wipe your face, chickabiddy. I can't talk to somebody making that sort of noise."

Gemma sat up and took the face flannel. She scrubbed at her face and it helped. She stopped crying and all that was left was an occasional sniff and hiccup.

"Did Ann tell you?"

"She did." Alice sat down on the bed. "I don't accept that the school's reaction is as unkind as you think it will be." She saw Gemma was going to argue so she stopped

46

her. "No, let me finish. But if that is what you think, you will imagine all sorts of things happening that aren't happening at all."

Gemma was still looking miserable so Ann said:

"Mum's had an idea, Gemma."

Alice took one of Gemma's hands.

"I only told the school that we would have a niece living with us who would be coming as a pupil in the summer term, so they don't know who you are. My idea is that we switch you from being my niece to being Uncle Philip's."

Ann and Gemma looked puzzled.

"What good will that do?" Ann asked.

Her mother smiled.

"Just that it won't be Gemma Bow who goes to Headstone Comprehensive, it will be Gemma Robinson."

CHAPTER NINE: THE UNIFORM

ALICE told Lydia and Robin that Gemma had changed her surname.

"They'll have to know," she explained to Ann. "After all, the young brothers and sisters of the pupils at your school are at their school. If by chance one of them should mention Gemma we don't want Lydia and Robin saying 'But her name's Bow, not Robinson.'"

Alice told the younger two very casually just as if changing your surname was something that happened every day. It was in the kitchen while she was clearing away breakfast, supposedly helped by Lydia and Robin.

"By the way, Gemma's using our surname at school."

"Why?" asked Lydia.

"It's easier one lot of marking tapes for everybody. Look what yards I bought with Robinson on it."

"I'm not sure I like her using our name," said Lydia. "She's been fairly all right so far, but I've a feeling she might show off any minute."

Alice would have liked to say "Don't worry, she won't. She doesn't want anybody to know who she is." But it was unlikely Lydia, if she knew the truth, could be relied on to keep it to herself. So instead she laughed.

"Don't be such a goose. By the time she's in her school uniform she'll be like one pea in a pod."

Talking of uniform reminded Robin of his troubles.

"I know, as I'm having all new uniform when I go to St. Giles, it's silly to buy anything new for now but my shorts are much too tight, they pinch."

"That'll be all right," Alice said. "We're much better off now that Gemma's here. Aunt Rowena is paying very generously, far more than she costs to keep. Anyway, you'll want clothes other than your school uniform for holidays. I'm taking Gemma to buy her uniform this afternoon so you can come, too, and we'll buy your shorts at the same time."

Lydia had been practising a few foot exercises. Now she stopped.

"Talking of buying. I do most awfully need a new cardigan for after dancing. All I've got to put on over my tunic when it's cold is my school blazer. Lots of the girls have pink cardigans to match their belts."

Alice was not easily caught out by Lydia.

"I must come to one of your Saturday lessons and have a look. I shouldn't think you'd be the only child wrongly dressed."

"I never said I was the only one, there are others, what I said was school blazers aren't worn, especially not by a person like me who's got a scholarship."

Robin looked disgusted.

"You get more conceited every day, Lydie."

Lydia, still drying a cup, moved to the end of the room where there was room for her to turn a pirouette.

"You get more conceited every day, Lydie"
49

"It's not conceit, my poor boy, it's just facing facts. I have got a scholarship and I can dance."

"Well, I've got a scholarship," Robin protested, "but I don't yap about it all day long."

Alice thought it quite possible Lydia did need a cardigan. If school blazers were considered infra dig it was only too likely when she was hot and she should put something on she wouldn't do it.

"Don't dance when you're drying up, Lydie. I thought we'd all go shopping this afternoon and as it's almost the end of the holidays we'd have tea in the shop afterwards."

"Good!" said Robin. "That's where you get cinnamon toast."

Gemma was secretly dismayed when she heard all the family were coming to the shop where her uniform was to be bought, but she could say nothing as they were going out to tea afterwards.

"While we're at the shop," her aunt explained, "Robin needs shorts so I thought we'd kill two birds with one stone."

"Three birds," said Lydia. "I need a cardigan for my dancing." She turned to Gemma. "I expect you learnt dancing in London, didn't you, so you know school blazers aren't worn?"

Gemma, between films, had learnt various subjects that might help her. Fencing, dancing and singing. "You never know," her mother had said, "you might get an offer for a musical, anyway, the fencing and dancing will help your figure when you're older." But now, asked a straight question by Lydia, she did not want to admit too much. Her dancing had not been a bit like the sort Lydia was learning, and she was certain the singing wasn't in the Robinsons' class.

"Just a bit I did, but I could never go regularly because of pictures."

"Well, didn't you have a pink cardigan to put on when you got hot?" Lydia persisted.

Gemma had learnt all her outside subjects at a stage

school. Both for fencing and dancing the regular pupils had a uniform, but she had worn what she liked, usually shorts with a sleeveless top. But now she thought of it Miss Court had always carried a cardigan for her to put on if she rested. But she had so many clothes she had no idea what colour it had been, probably just the first one Miss Court took off the shelf. However, she couldn't say that sort of thing in front of the cousins.

"Yes, I did, I suppose, though I'm not sure it was pink." Then Gemma had an idea. "I've got lots of cardigans of all colours. Why don't you come and choose one? I'll never wear them all now I'm to wear uniform."

Lydia was charmed. And before her mother could protest she had seized Gemma's hand and was pulling her out of the room.

"Thank you. Thank you awfully. Let's choose one now."

Alice looked at Ann.

"We can't have too much of that. I know Gemma has a lot of clothes but she mustn't give them away, it's sweet of her but her mother chose them for her to wear."

Ann thought of the clothes bulging out of the cupboards, shelves and drawers.

"Call it lending," she suggested. "She's got too much and if she's going to be a Robinson she may as well learn to share."

Gemma wore the yellow outfit she had travelled in to go shopping. She looked, Alice thought, rather wistfully like a creature from another world beside her cousins. They were tidily and nicely dressed but they could not compete with Gemma's models from the latest boutiques for young girls. "Oh, well," she thought, "Ann and Lydia don't mind so why should I?"

The shop where the uniform was bought specialised in school uniforms. The assistant briskly measured Gemma, then from a drawer she flicked out two blouses, from a stand she fetched a grey pleated skirt and a purple blazer and laid a purple tie on the blouses. "Hats are downstairs," she said. "Better slip into one of the fitting-rooms, dear, and try the lot on and you want a bit of purple ribbon for that hair."

When Gemma had gone out shopping either with her mother or Miss Court she had received the undivided attention of at least one assistant. And often, as frocks were brought out and held against her, there had been oohs and aahs from other assistants. And when she had been smaller she had sometimes modelled children's dresses for coloured supplements and magazines. "This dress was specially designed for little Gemma Bow." So it was hard to take when she was told to slip into a fitting-room; obviously to the assistant she was just one of hundreds of girls no better and no worse—just ordinary.

Helped by Ann and Lydia, for Alice had gone with Robin to buy his shorts, the yellow outfit came off and the new clothes were put on. To Gemma the blouse felt as if it was made of cardboard.

"It scratches," she said. "Does the blouse have to be made of this stuff?"

Gemma held out the tie.

"It will be all right when it's washed. They're marvellous really, you just rinse them out overnight and they come out like new in the morning. Imagine if we had blouses we had to iron!"

Gemma despondently put the tie round her neck and Ann tied it for her.

"There's a brooch with the school badge we pin on it. You buy them at school."

"Put on the skirt," said Lydia. "They aren't bad."

The skirts were well pleated and were quite nice but Gemma thought the length wrong.

"This is too long."

Ann stood away from Gemma to see her better.

"It's about right. They are supposed just to touch the knee. Of course they never do because we grow, and anyway lots of girls hitch them up. But most of us start with them the right length."

Gemma had just got the blazer on when her aunt and Robin came back.

"My goodness! " said Robin. "You look almost exactly like Ann looks in term time."

"Except for the hair." Alice came to Gemma and held her hair back. "Now look in the glass, Gemma. It isn't too bad, is it?"

Gemma looked and could scarcely believe what she saw. To her she looked a caricature of all the schoolgirls in the country. There was not a sign of Gemma Bow left. She could have cried. Instead she bowed to her image in the looking-glass.

"Exit Gemma Bow," she said. "Enter Gemma Robinson."

CHAPTER TEN: UNCLE PHILIP

PHILIP ROBINSON, though he never complained, was finding his life in the orchestra library difficult. As a musician with The Steen he had lived in a world he loved and understood. The world of rehearsals and performances which, wherever The Steen played, followed the same pattern. He had little to be responsible for except to get himself and his fiddle to the right place at the right time. All the arrangements were made by others: their manager had the tickets for flights and trains and when they were abroad he even took charge of the passports.

In the music library, because he was supernumerary to the regular staff, he was expected, it seemed to him, to be responsible for every sheet of music in the library. Others had regular jobs, like replacing or repairing torn sheets, but it was he who had to search when one sheet of music was wrongly filed. It was he who had to check and recheck all the music required for a concert or, worse still, a tour. Not that he minded the work, he was grateful for it and grateful to be amongst music, but when someone shouted "Robinson, isn't that stuff checked yet?" he felt humiliated. Wryly he quoted to himself a saying his mother was fond of: "Pride comes before a fall." But had he been proud? Not proud, he thought, just happy.

Because he knew how it felt when fate demoted you he watched Gemma with sympathy. When Alice had told him Gemma wanted to be called Robinson he had surprised her by saying he thought it was a good idea.

Alice had showed her surprise.

"Do you? I wasn't sure it was the right thing to do. She's led such an unreal life I thought a bit of coming down to earth wouldn't hurt her. I only suggested changing her name because I hate the child to be unhappy."

Philip had wondered why it should be thought good for anybody to be bumped down to earth, but he had said nothing for he was the sort person who, as a rule, kept what he thought to himself. But he watched Gemma and thought about her and what he saw worried him.

Gemma had by nature an aloof, wistful charm which had made her a star, but after she started going to school it seemed to him that she had a look of permanent unhappiness. Without being too obvious about it he tried to discover what was wrong. He started by questioning Ann.

"How is Gemma making out at school?"

They were alone in the sitting-room for Alice was in the kitchen, Lydia in the bathroom practising her dancing, Robin outside in the street with friends and Gemma in her bedroom finishing her homework. It was Ann's week to lay the table. She put down a pile of plates.

"All right I think. I don't see much of her but she never says anything is wrong."

"I thought you were in the same class."

Ann came to him and sat on the arm of his chair.

"Well, we are sort of. I mean we are both in the first class but at the Comprehensive classes are divided into three. I'm in form 1.U. She is in 1.E."

"Does that mean she is above you?"

"No. Actually she does easier work. The initials are our class teacher's. She is Ursula Sheila End. So we have a 1.U.—that's me. 1.S. and 1.E.—that's Gemma."

Philip thought about that.

"I suppose really it's A, B and C."

Ann nodded.

"I suppose so, but calling us U. S. and E. is supposed not to make anyone feel inferior. It happens all up the school. Not those particular letters but always three, mostly chosen from the name of the teacher."

"Is Gemma stupid?"

"Oh no, I don't think so. I think she just hasn't done much lessons." Ann went back to her table laying. "That Miss Court who was her governess never made her work. I think very likely she'll catch up because at some things she's very good. She likes English literature, she's read much more than I have."

"So if she gets on she might join you later on?"

"I suppose so, I don't know much about how it works because I've only done two terms, and, of course, the older ones never talk to us in the first class. But it may be difficult for Gemma to catch up because she knows almost nothing about some of the most important subjects."

"Such as?"

"Arithmetic for one, she says she hated it so Miss Court didn't often make her do it. Imagine, Dad, she can only just add and subtract."

Philip smiled.

"She has a bit of the way to go if she is to get on to higher mathematics, which I suppose you learn at the top of the school."

Ann had finished laying the things she had brought in. She turned to the door to fetch another tray full.

"If it comes to that I've a bit of a way to go too. It frightens me to think of all there is to learn."

Philip seldom saw Gemma alone. By the time he got home Ann and Gemma were deep in their homework.

It was a rule that all books were away by 8.30 when Alice gave both the girls mugs of hot chocolate. While they drank it sometimes they watched television or they played a game or talked. They were always a foursome at chocolate time for Lydia and Robin were in bed.

Then one Saturday when Alice had taken Lydia and Robin to a party and Ann was at an extra choir practice Philip got his chance. It was a lovely day so they were sitting on the lawn. Gemma had just written to her mother and as she licked round the edges of the overseas letter he said:

"Are you getting used to being at school?"

Gemma was caught off guard. Uncle Philip was not a person who seemed to like talking, she had expected to read her book when her letter was finished.

"I suppose so. I mean I've learned my way round now. It took me simply ages, it's such a big building."

"And are you liking it?"

He spoke so interestedly, as if he really wanted to know, that Gemma answered him truthfully.

"I loathe it. You can't be lower than form 1.E. We're not supposed to think that but I do. We are always having pep talks about how in Comprehensive Schools everybody gets the same chance and so how much better it is than the old way when there were secondary moderns and grammar schools. But I should think that's just talk. I know I'm in what the teachers call the C stream. That means the stupid ones. Well, if that's what I'm going to be, I bet I'd do better in a school which was all C stream. I mean, you would get a chance to shine."

"If it really is C stream I expect you can rise. First to B and then to A."

"I suppose I might but it's particularly difficult for me. You see, I'm no earthly good at mathematics."

"Aren't you? But I would take a bet your I.Q. is high."

"Would you?" Gemma looked pleased. "I've got so used to thinking no one could be nearer a worm than me

56

that it's quite hard to remember people used to think I was bright."

"You'll have to let them know who you are some-time."

Gemma looked appalled.

"Oh no! Every night in my prayers I say 'Thank you, God, for letting me hide behind the name of Robinson.' As Gemma Robinson I can just bear being me but as Gemma Bow I couldn't."

"But you'll have to use your talents some time. I suppose they do plays at your school."

"If they do they'd never look in 1.E. for talent."

Philip refused to accept that.

"Ann is only in form 1 but she sings in the choir and is being picked for a soloist I believe."

"That's different. Ann is in 1.U. That's the A stream. When you are in that you can get anywhere. Anyway, they heard about her concerts and things. If I sang at concerts I suppose, even though I'm in 1.E., they just might put me in the choir. My goodness, it would put my stock up if they did because, for special things like that, you get marks for your house. But you see I don't sing at concerts."

Her uncle thought that over.

"I'm sure humility is a great virtue," he said at last, "but I doubt if too much of it brings out the best in most of us."

Gemma was surprised for that did not sound the sort of thing you would expect an uncle to say.

"Fancy you thinking that, for it's what I think all the time."

"Well, you and I are rather in the same boat. I dare-say to you to be a first fiddle in The Steen seems unimportant but to musicians it means a lot."

Gemma had not thought about her uncle's career at all. She knew he had played with The Steen and, of course, she had heard of The Steen for everybody had. She knew he had rheumatism or something in his hands and had been ordered to rest them, and that was why he was working in the music library. But that he felt he, too, had come down in the world was an entirely new thought. Then she looked at him and knew he was quite right. He did understand how she felt, not because he tried to, like Ann and Aunt Alice did, but because he was being hurt in the same way.

"There's nothing we can do about it. I expect it gets easier when you are more used to it."

Again her uncle thought over what Gemma had said.

"I wouldn't say there was nothing you could do about it. It's difficult for me for what I need is patience and faith that my hands will recover. I should have thought there was plenty you could do. If you're right about the low status of class 1.E. I'd do something to show the rest of the school that you are not as dull as they think you are."

"But I am a dumb cluck. There are terrible holes in my education."

"I was thinking more of outside subjects. How about music?"

"Good gracious, no! I made a record when I was very small of a song about me and a kitten, but it wasn't singing like Ann and Robin sing." Gemma smiled. "The only music I can do at all you wouldn't approve of. I had to play the banjo in one picture so I had lessons. I loved that but I had to give it up because we couldn't make time."

"Banjo! You don't meet them so often these days, it's mostly electric guitars. I could arrange for you to have lessons if you liked. Why shouldn't Miss Gemma Robinson be the best banjo player in the school?"

At once Gemma felt quite different. Though she had not known it she had wished that she had a special interest like the others had. Of course, she had acting but you couldn't do that by yourself.

"Oh, please do find someone to teach me." Gemma hesitated. "And I had been thinking I'd like to go on with my dancing. I don't do ballet like Lydie but I suppose there's a class for people who want to learn tap and things like that."

"Sure to be. We'll get Lydie to make enquiries."

Gemma lay back in her chair feeling more at ease than she had felt since she came to the house. She would learn the banjo and work at it and work at it. Then, when she thought she was good enough, she would let people hear her play.

"Wouldn't it be odd," she said, "if I could make the name Gemma Robinson mean something! "

CHAPTER ELEVEN: TOFFEE

Lydia had been promoted to one private lesson a week with Miss Arrowhead. What she learnt at these classes nobody knew for Lydia refused to discuss them.

"Just Miss Arrowhead's things," she would say.

When she was told to enquire about classes for Gemma she said she would ask Miss Arrowhead after her next private class.

"I don't think she teaches the sort of dancing you want," she told Gemma. "She thinks all dancers should be ballet trained and then you can dance anything."

"Well, I don't mind learning ballet," Gemma said. "It will have to be a beginners' class because I've never done any."

Lydia nodded.

"You'll start with Polly. Anyway, I'll tell Miss Arrowhead about you."

Alice overheard this.

"But she'll still be Gemma Robinson remember. It's no good her having two names."

Lydia shrugged her shoulders.

"Pity. I'd like to have told Miss Arrowhead who you

really are. Not that she's interested in films, music is her thing. She goes to every concert The Steen give."

Lydia's special class was on Wednesday after school. So the next Wednesday, after her lesson, having bobbed to Miss Arrowhead—which was how every class finished—she came over to her.

"We have a cousin staying with us. Her name is Gemma. She is eleven and she has learnt a sort of dancing in London. She had a governess called Miss Court who taught her. I don't mind telling you Miss Court sounds an awful idiot to me. Anyway, she took Gemma to her classes."

"Where did Gemma learn?" Miss Arrowhead asked.

"It was a stage school called The Ambassadors, but she only went there for fencing and dancing and then not all the time. I mean sometimes she was too busy to go."

Miss Arrowhead looked amused.

"What was Gemma so busy at?"

Too late Lydia saw she had said too much.

"Things. I mean I don't know exactly. Anyway, now she wants to learn dancing. Not our sort but tap and things like that. But she said if you didn't have a class for tap she'd start with ballet. I told her she'd learn with Polly."

Miss Arrowhead felt Lydia was hiding something from her. Knowing about Philip being unable to play in the orchestra she wondered if again the trouble was money. But surely, if the Robinsons were hard up, they would not take on an extra child unless she could pay.

"I expect Gemma can start with Polly," she agreed. "Anyway, I'll telephone your mother tonight. Now run along and change."

Miss Arrowhead, when she telephoned, had other subjects to talk to Alice about than Gemma.

"Of course, much can go wrong but if Lydie continues to improve as she is at the moment I think you may have a dancer in the family. In the autumn I should like to take her for individual lessons three times a week as well as in my general class on Saturdays."

"It's very good of you," said Alice. "And I'm glad to say we can afford to pay for at least the general class. My sister pays us well to have my niece Gemma living with us."

Miss Arrowhead laughed.

"Oh yes—the busy Gemma who has not had time to attend regular classes. At least that is what Lydie told me. I think the Saturday class will suit her to start with. If she wants to learn tap later on I know a place where she can go for lessons."

"Let's see how she gets on with Polly's class to start with," said Alice. "Can she start next Saturday? I'll send you a cheque right away."

"Thank you." Miss Arrowhead was about to ring off when she remembered something. "By the way, what's Gemma's surname?"

Alice hated lying to Miss Arrowhead.

"Robinson."

At the other end of the line Miss Arrowhead, as she put down the receiver, frowned in a puzzled way.

"How odd that Mrs. Robinson's sister's child should be called Robinson. Oh well, perhaps Mr. Robinson married his cousin."

Although it was comforting to be learning the banjo and being able to tell yourself someday you'd show them all how clever you were, inside Gemma felt more and more humiliated. As a result, as the summer term progressed, she grew more and more rebellious. She was so used to being in the centre of the picture that it was endlessly grating to find herself so far in the background that she didn't show at all. Then one day, quite by accident, she discovered that if she could not shine anywhere else she could in her own class. She had gone to the sweetshop to buy some chocolate to eat mid-morning. Mrs. Gag, who ran the shop, was unpacking some treacle toffee.

"I don't know what they think they're up to," she said. "Maybe your young teeth can take it but I thought my National Health set were glued up for good." Mrs. Gag held out the box. "Have a piece so you'll see what I mean."

Gemma took one of the toffees and put it in her mouth. Mrs. Gag was right, the toffee was real lockjaw stuff. Her teeth were so firmly held together she couldn't even thank Mrs. Gag. She could only giggle and make faces. However, violent sucking released her teeth at last and she decided it would be fun to buy some and glue up all the cousins. Then, just as Mrs. Gag was weighing out the toffee, she had another and, she thought, brilliant idea. She would buy enough for all her class at school and she would hand it round before English Literature, which usually started with reading out loud.

"I shall want thirty-eight pieces," she said as best she could through the toffee. "It's for my class at school, there are thirty-eight of us."

Mrs. Gag laughed as she counted the toffees into her weighing machine.

"Been talking too much, have they, dear? Well, this'll be your only chance to buy this sort for I'm sending it back. I reckon these are a special batch cooked wrong for usually they come hard and crisp."

The English Literature lesson came after morning break. Before the class began Gemma nipped from desk to desk murmuring "Have a toffee". Nobody refused for nobody suspected Gemma, so far they had thought of her as quiet and rather dull. Just as Gemma had finished handing round the toffee Ursula End, the teacher, came in.

"Open your books," she said, "at page eight. Now, before we discuss the poem, we will hear it again." She looked at a boy in the back row. "John, will you read the first verse, please."

John moved his jaws and struggled to open his mouth but not a sound came out. Puzzled, Ursula left him alone.

"John doesn't seem able to read the verse." She turned to a girl. "You read it, Sally."

Sally was, of course, in the same position, she struggled

hard to speak but all that came out was "Psst!" which was as near as she could get to saying please.

It took no time for Ursula to grasp what the trouble must be.

"It's disgraceful," she said. "You know you are forbidden to eat sweets in class. You have just had break, why didn't you finish your sweets then? Remember this sort of behaviour is taken into account when you are marked for the House Cup. If it happens again I shall fine you several points."

The whole school were grouped into houses called after famous authors. The house with the highest number of points for work and play in any year was awarded the House Cup, so at this awful threat of being fined points there were toffee-smothered groans. For to lose points for your house was a fearful disgrace.

"I shall read the poem to you," said Ursula, "and when I have finished I hope you will all have swallowed whatever sweet it is you are chewing. This once I shall let the matter pass but if it happens again you know what to expect."

By the time Ursula had read the poem the toffee was dissolving and, though rather indistinctly, the children were able to answer the questions she put to them.

Gemma waited nervously for the end of morning school. What would the class say to her for getting them all into trouble? But that was where she had her surprise. For the moment they got into the playground the children gathered round her, slapping her on the back.

"Good old Gemma!" "I say, what a jibe!" "Old End was savage, wasn't she, but what could she do about it?" "I was dying to laugh but I couldn't because of my teeth being stuck." "Good old Gemma!" "Good old Gemma!"

To be admired! To be good old Gemma again! It was like having a meal after you had been desperately hungry. Gemma's heart sang "They like me. They like me, and not because of my acting but me, Gemma Robinson."

On the way home she told Ann what had happened.

Not what the class had said afterwards but just about the toffee. Ann did not think it funny.

"What an idiotic thing to do! Suppose Miss End had made a thing of it and found out it was you?"

Gemma, still feeling the pats on her back and hearing the "Good old Gemmas", was not going to be deflated.

"I wouldn't have cared. She ought to have enough sense of humour to see it's funny."

"I don't see why she should," said Ann. "When you like English Literature like she does and have only three-quarters of an hour to teach it in, it wouldn't be funny if no one could speak because of toffee."

Gemma danced on ahead.

"I don't care what she thought, I thought it funny and, if you want to know, so did every single person in the class."

CHAPTER TWELVE: MAKING YOUR MARK

HAVING tasted class popularity Gemma longed for more. It took her no time to find out how to get it. It was easy for her, trained in the use of words and inflections, to bait the teachers with answers which sounded harmless but could also be read as rude. Eagerly her rather sheep-like classmates tried to follow suit, but without Gemma's talent the rudeness was usually detected and they got into trouble. Soon it became unpopular in the class if you worked well and tried hard. "Teachers' pet," was a phrase to be dreaded, for it was surprising, in spite of supervision, how you could get knocked about in the playground.

Gemma was full of ideas.

"Let's all put our grammars underneath the other books in our desks, then, when Miss End says: 'Open your grammar books' we'll all open our desks at once. Let's

64

see who can be longest looking. I'll give a Mars bar to the winner."

Gemma would think up different words for the song they were learning at singing class. They weren't really excruciatingly funny words but most of the class thought they were and were suffocated with giggles, which drove the music teacher mad.

At gym, taught by the sports' mistress, there were, Gemma discovered, a variety of ways of being irritating. One day no one in the class knew their left leg from their right.

"I'm sorry, Miss Sparrow. I never can remember which is which."

And it was child's play to mess up marching. One or two pupils turning the wrong way and the march was a shambles.

Then one day Gemma thought up the serial story. This was to fill up dull patches, such as arithmetic and geography lessons. The stories were poor efforts in the James Bond style but 1.E. thought them splendid. The hero was called Lancelot Panther and to them he was gorgeous. His story was written in an exercise book and went on from day to day. The game was to pass the book to your neighbour without the teacher seeing. Then the recipient read through the day's instalment as far as it had gone before writing their own instalment, then passing the book to the next desk. Even those children who refused to join in had not the nerve not to receive the book and pass it on. It kept the class in a constant state of suppressed excitement for especially, as in the forward rows, it was very difficult to pass or write in the book undetected, and in the front rows it was impossible. As a result, when the book was in the forward part of the classroom, the back rows were continually bobbing up and down to see where it had got to.

In the common room Ursula came in for a lot of questioning.

C

"What's the matter with your kids in 1.E., Ursula? They're savages."

"Why is there no trouble with 1.U. and 1.S. but it's hell let loose when one tries to teach 1.E.?"

"If I could arrange it I'd put all your little dears in 1.E. in a bus, Ursula, and tip it over a cliff."

Poor Ursula would admit that 1.E. certainly were out of hand.

"There must be a ringleader whom they are running after like sheep, but which is it? Individually they look as if butter wouldn't melt in their mouths."

"But, Miss End," said the headmaster, Mr. Stevens, "if you are looking for a ringleader it shouldn't be so difficult. 1.E. were all right last term, weren't they?"

"Yes."

"Well, who are new this term?"

"I've thought about that. There's that boy, Paul Perkins, who was placed in 1.S. but couldn't keep up, and a cousin of a girl in 1.U. called Gemma Robinson."

"Cousin of Ann Robinson who sings?"

"That's her. A quiet little thing with a sad, wistful face. I'm sure she'd never be a ringleader."

"I'm certain you'll find there is a leader. A class seldom gets out of hand on its own, someone is setting them off. Keep a watch on Paul and Gemma, you never know, the quietest child can surprise you."

Meanwhile, at her Saturday dancing class, Gemma was a model of good behaviour, the reason being that she enjoyed her lesson and she liked Polly and being in the studio. Polly never treated children in a lump, to her each was an individual. When she deserved it Gemma was praised, for, though she was a beginner, she was used to being directed and so was easy to teach. She listened and took in what she was told to do and then, to the best of her ability, did it. So quite often Polly would say:

"Don't all start moving before I tell you what I want you to do. Now watch Gemma, her feet may not be quite

ight, nor her position, but she does know exactly what I
have told her to do."

"It's funny about Gemma, that cousin of Lydie's," she
told Miss Arrowhead. "She is a beginner at dancing but
she seems experienced somehow, like a professional. I was
giving the children a bit of mime the other day—very
simple. They were supposed to be in a market in Italy. I
gave each of them a character. Gemma was a beggar.
'You have a begging bowl in your left hand,' I said, 'the
right hand is for the money,' and I showed her where to
move and so on. Do you know, when we started miming
she became a beggar and she made no mistakes, she held
the bowl exactly as I had told her. Some of the other children weren't bad but each of them had to say: 'Oh, Polly,
I forgot' about something, but not Gemma. I'm sure
there's a bit of the pro in her."

"I must come and have a look at her," said Miss Arrowhead. "Lydie's coming on wonderfully, I daren't even
think about it, but wouldn't it be a thrill if, after teaching
all these years, I should have found a winner!"

Gemma gave no trouble either at her banjo lessons. Her
uncle had found a young man called Ted Smith to teach
her. He had been a pupil of his own and was really a
violinist but, like most musicians, he could play several
instruments. Gemma liked him on sight, he had a cheerful grin and, though he taught music in a school, he
seemed to her the sort of person who might have been a
floor manager in a film studio, he had the same sort of
easy, friendly way with him.

"I understand you've had a lesson or two, why did you
give it up?"

Gemma had thought of an answer to that.

"Mummy and I were moving about."

"What do you want to do, play properly or be able to
pick out the accompaniment for songs?"

"Quite truthfully, Mr. Smith," said Gemma, "I don't
think I'm musical enough to play anything really well. I

don't sing much but I'd like to be able to accompany myself."

"Right then, that's what we'll aim at. And you needn't call me Mr. Smith—Ted will do. It's not a bad moment to learn, for with this revival of folk music, there are some good songs about."

Ted came to the house to teach her. He came after school on Wednesdays, which was a good time for Ann had choir practice and Lydia a dancing class, and he came on Saturday mornings after she had finished her dancing lesson, and she managed to practise most days so she got on nicely.

"In about four months," Ted told her, "you'll be able to say you can play."

What with enjoying her dancing and banjo lessons, and plotting new ways of showing her class how to make a nuisance of themselves, Gemma was finding life fun. She lost the unhappy look she had worn when she had first come and the real Gemma came out. The Gemma whom the film studios had known.

In May the girls of the school were told they could wear their cotton dresses. These were mauve and white check made in any design the girls fancied. Alice had made Ann's two frocks at home, they were quite nice though Gemma thought them a bit dowdy. Gemma was sent to a dressmaker for hers and, except in length, they were in the latest fashion. Although she thought her hair looked awful tied back she was pleased with herself the first day she wore one of the new frocks. So it was in a cheerful state of mind that she arrived at school. What could be pleasanter than to know you looked nice and that all your class were going to say "Good old Gemma."?

But when Gemma marched with her class into her classroom after prayers she felt at once that something was wrong, and she was certain of it when Ursula said:

"I'm making a change in the seating. I want Paul Perkins and Gemma Robinson to move into these two desks in the front row." She smiled at the two present owners of the front desks. "And you two will move to the back to Gemma and Paul's desks."

While collecting her books, behind the upturned lid of her desk, Gemma made expressive faces to her neighbours. Her face said: "How am I going to organize things sitting under Miss End's nose?" But the class were nervous and Gemma got no answering looks.

"Cowards!" she thought. "I'll show them." She shut down her desk top and with her arms full of books marched down to her new desk in the middle of the front row.

Miss End looked at Gemma and her face was thoughtful.

CHAPTER THIRTEEN: ONE HUNDRED LINES

GEMMA despised her classmates. "A lot of silly sheep," she thought, for without her to lead them they at once fell back into their old docile ways. Whatever she had planned she had always been the first to carry out, whether it was writing about Launcelot Panther or shooting the front of the class with an indiarubber sprung off a ruler. But from the middle of the front row she could start nothing.

"You are a lot of idiots," she grumbled in the playground.

"You can pass Launcelot Panther round without me."

"But you can't write in the book," one of the boys pointed out. "Nobody can in the front row."

Gemma looked defiant.

"Who says I can't? You start passing it round and you'll see. It can't pass along the front row but give my desk a kick when it's behind me and I'll take it that way."

"But you couldn't write in it," one of the girls argued. "Miss End would be bound to see."

"Why?" Gemma asked. "I'll write in it while she's writing on the blackboard."

It took several lesson periods for the Launcelot Panther saga to pass round the class but, urged by Gemma, it again began to circulate cautiously. By the afternoon it had reached the row of desks behind Gemma's. It was French, the last lesson of the day. Excitement was at fever heat. Would Gemma really dare to take the book and write in it under Miss End's very nose?

Ursula could feel that the class were excited about something and it was clear from some very confused answering that their minds were not on French verbs. But what? Whatever was going on was clearly nothing to do with the two new children—Paul and Gemma. The headmaster had been wrong about that. Poor Paul was, as usual, quite out of his depth. He was a borderline case for a special school. Gemma looked a picture of how a good schoolgirl should look, her frock was spotless and her hair, neatly tied back, shone. "Perhaps more like an advertisement for how a schoolgirl should look than how they really do," Ursula thought.

Towards the finish of the class Gemma's seat was kicked. She could not move at that moment for Miss End was facing her. Then, when she turned to the blackboard, quick as lightning, Gemma put her hands behind her back and into them was pushed Launcelot Panther's exercise book.

Ursula turned round.

"Now copy down what I have written on the blackboard for this is your homework for tonight."

Gemma moved Launcelot Panther into her left hand and, holding the exercise book behind her back, picked up her pen with her right hand and began copying what was on the blackboard. It's not easy on a desk to write without holding on to the book or paper on which you are writing. And though Gemma was careful the book slipped slightly sideways and she had no free hand to straighten it.

Ursula saw this.

"Hold your book, Gemma, it will be much easier."

Gemma knew the whole class was holding its breath.

"I'm resting my left hand. I think I've strained it."

Ursula smelt a rat.

"Well, that's no way to rest it holding it behind your back. Let me look at it."

Gemma tried to push Launcelot Panther on to the seat behind her but she missed it and the book fell to the floor. But Gemma was not an actress for nothing. Apparently unmoved she held out her left hand.

"The swelling's gone down but it has been painful."

Ursula stepped off her dais and came to Gemma's desk. She appeared to look at the hand.

"It certainly seems all right now." Then she stooped and picked up Launcelot Panther. She opened it. There was a pause in which, had a drawing-pin dropped, it would have sounded like a bomb. Then she read out the opening lines.

"Launcelot Panther, looking gorgeous, stepped into his Rolls-Royce car. The car was purple and the chauffeur wore a purple uniform. 'Take me to Scotland Yard,' Launcelot Panther said."

Ursula turned over the pages.

"This opus would appear to be a class effort. When was it written?"

"Oh, just any time," said Gemma.

"In class no doubt. I see by the handwriting you wrote those memorable first lines which I have just read. Was the idea of writing this story"—she turned the book over to read the title—"Launcelot Panther, Secret Agent, yours?"

It was obvious it was no good lying.

"Yes."

Ursula looked round the class. A book like this passing from hand to hand would explain the lack of attention

71

of which she and the other teachers had complained. If Gemma had thought this up, for how much more was she responsible?

"I shall set the whole class an extra page of French to be done with your homework tonight. But you, Gemma, will stay behind after class. You lied to me about your sprained hand. I will not be lied to so you will write me a hundred lines."

Gemma wondered for a second if anyone would protest that it wasn't fair to punish her specially as they were all to blame, but she was not surprised when nobody said a word. Meekly, looking, as Ursula told the common room later, the picture of innocence, Gemma said:

"My cousin Ann and I are supposed to walk home together. We meet after school."

Ursula was not caught.

"That cannot happen every day for Ann sings in the choir and all choir practices are after school." She looked round for a responsible messenger. "Sally, will you find Ann Robinson after school and tell her not to wait for Gemma."

Gemma hated that. Ann was not exactly a teacher's pet but she liked school and always worked hard. Next to her singing, to her the most important thing was working for House points. She wouldn't say anything at home about Gemma being kept in, she wasn't that sort, anyway there were only Lydia and Robin to tell for she would be home before Aunt Alice got back from the hospital, and long before Uncle Philip came home from the music library. But if she told Ann what it was all about she wouldn't see that writing Launcelot Panther had been fun, and stirring up the class exciting. She would just think she was silly, she might even think she ought to feel ashamed. There was one good thing about Ann, she wouldn't let Sally tell her what it was about. Almost Gemma could hear her shutting Sally up. "Gemma will tell me, thank you."

The class came to an end and, sobered by the page of extra French, the children trooped out. Not one of them gave Gemma a sympathising glance. No one looked as if they were thinking "Good old Gemma."

Ursula put a piece of lined paper on Gemma's desk.

"Write out a hundred times 'I have made a fool of myself'."

Gemma's head shot up and colour flooded her cheeks.

"I thought it was because you thought I was telling a lie I was to be punished. I don't think I've made a fool of myself."

"Start writing, you may feel differently by the time you have finished."

Half an hour later, Gemma, stretching her cramped thumb and first finger, did feel a little different. To be alone with Miss End, with no sound but her turning over pages as she corrected books, did seem to have taken some of the spirit out of her. She looked up.

"I've finished."

While apparently hard at work correcting books Ursula had been thinking about Gemma. She had evidently found the ringleader who was leading the class astray, but why was Gemma doing it? That sort of naughtiness was often a type of showing off. Usually it was a deprived child who found it necessary to show off. She was realising how little she knew about Gemma. She didn't look like a deprived child in any way, but was she? She was parked out with cousins, did that mean there had been a break-up of her home?

"Bring the paper to me, Gemma."

Gemma climbed on to the dais and laid her paper in front of Ursula.

"It's not very neat, is it?" Ursula said.

"I don't think anybody could be neat as well as writing the same thing a hundred times," Gemma protested.

"Has it been fun making a nuisance of yourself?" Ursula asked.

Gemma wished she could see Miss End's face. Why was she asking that? Did she know she had done more than get the class writing Launcelot Panther?

"How do you mean?"

"You know very well what I mean. This may not be a very bright class but it was well-behaved until you joined it."

"But dull," said Gemma. "Dreadfully, dreadfully dull. I do hate dullness."

She spoke with such fervour that Ursula was interested.

"Are you finding it dull at Headstone?"

"Not Headstone exactly and I like living with the cousins, and there's things I learn outside I like, but I simply hate this school."

Ursula struggled to remember what had been on Gemma's entry form.

"You were educated privately until you came here, weren't you?"

"Yes. I had a governess."

Alice had carefully left this bit of information off the entrance form. She knew the surprise it would cause for who, today, had a governess? Not even royalty.

"A governess. Wasn't that dull?"

Gemma thought of Miss Court. Kind, admiring Miss Court. But it was impossible to say lessons with her were exciting, and she could not tell Miss End that her lessons weren't exciting but film work was, especially when she went on location to interesting places.

"Yes, it was. But I feel worse here because of being in 1.E. You can't sink lower, can you?"

You couldn't and it had often worried Ursula lest the children felt this. She knew it was desperately important they should not feel C stream even if they were. Now Gemma had said how she felt it gave her a chance to speak out as she felt.

"Then climb out of it. I think you are an intelligent child."

"I'm a dumb cluck at mathematics."

"You'll catch up if you work. Why don't you try, Gemma? All right, you don't like 1.E. Well, move up then to 1.S. and then join your cousin in 1.U."

"Do you think I could?"

"I know you could. And, believe me, if you work with an aim like that you won't find school dull."

A new picture swam before Gemma. Gemma the brain. Gemma, who didn't get stuck in the bottom stream, but who climbed out.

She grinned at Ursula.

"I don't know if I can do it but I'd like to and I'm going to try."

"Good," said Ursula. "I shall be watching you."

CHAPTER FOURTEEN: AFTERMATH

In bed that night Gemma told Ann all that had happened.

"As a matter of fact I'm not sorry giving up planning things for the class to do. It was hard going for they got scared so easily. After all, what could anyone do to us?"

That startled Ann. She sat up.

"What could they do to you? Frightful things. A hundred lines is nothing. Why, you could lose House points. You only have three a term and to lose even one is a terrible disgrace."

"I don't mind about the House."

"That's because you don't understand," said Ann. "I'm in Dickens' House and, do you know, when I joined the choir a girl in the sixth congratulated me! Imagine how you'd feel if you lost points for Jane Austen, which is your house, and the girl in that part of the sixth who is captain of your House came and told you off."

Gemma thought about that.

"Quite truthfully I wouldn't care."

"I bet you would if it happened. I've never seen it but they say if you do a bit of work really carelessly, you know,

75

when you've no excuse like not understanding, you can get a big red R marked in your book. That means returned and you've not only got to do it again but you lose a House point. I'm terrified it will happen to me, I think I'd die of shame if it did."

Gemma could not see what Ann was getting worked up about.

"If I work hard so as to get moved into 1.S. I shan't get any big red Rs. But if I did I suppose I'd be angry with myself for having done badly when I was trying to do well, but I wouldn't mind about the point."

"There's a worse punishment than a red R." Ann lowered her voice. "There is the chair."

"What's that?"

"It's that big black chair. You must have seen it, it's in the middle of the school outside Mr. Stevens, the headmaster's office. If a pupil is rude or damages school property on purpose they can be sent to sit in the chair."

Gemma wanted to laugh.

"That doesn't sound too awful."

"It's a terrible disgrace. When Mr. Stevens comes out of his room, if he finds someone sitting in the chair, he asks why they are there and then he lectures them. It's quite public, anyone who happens to be about can hear the lecture and see who is getting it."

Gemma remembered how often she had been nearly rude. She certainly would not like the humiliation of sitting in the black chair. She must be careful in future. But she was not telling Ann she had ever been rude.

"I've only seen Mr. Stevens at prayers, he doesn't sound very fierce."

"They say he is if you are sent to the chair. A boy in 3.Y.—they are X, Y and Z in that class—was sent to it last term. He was thirteen and pretty tough but they say he was nearly crying when Mr. Stevens had done with him."

"Well," said Gemma, "I don't mean to be punished ever again. Now I'm going to work hard I shouldn't think

76

I ever would be. I know I've been rather bad so far, but that'll all be forgotten."

Ann lay down again for she was getting sleepy.

"I wouldn't count on that. Don't forget that most of the boys and girls in class 1. have younger brothers and sisters in the Junior Mixed. I bet somebody tells Lydie and Robin what happened to you."

Gemma did not like that. She did not want Lydia hearing she had been kept in to write a hundred lines.

"If Lydie has heard I'll ask her not to talk about it in front of Aunt Alice."

But Ann did not answer for she was asleep.

Ann was quite right. Lydia and Robin came back the next afternoon bursting with curiosity. While Ann was getting the tea they pestered Gemma with questions. Robin, laying the table, got in the first question.

"What did you have to write a hundred lines for? What had you done?"

Lydia was dancing round the living-room.

"In my class they said you had written about a murderer. Had you?"

Gemma sat down at the table.

"If I tell you what happened will you stop pestering me and will you promise not to talk about it when Uncle Philip and Aunt Alice come home?"

Lydia did a few dance steps.

"You can't read that, Gemma, but my feet promised. I remember better with my feet than with my head."

"I promise," said Robin. "I shouldn't have said anything anyway, I'm not a sneak."

So Gemma told them all about Launcelot Panther and how she had been made to write out "I have made a fool of myself."

Lydia held on to the door knob while she performed a demi-plié.

"I should have hated that and I think it was mean of your teacher to make you write it because it wasn't mak-

'And don't think you can start anything like that'

ing a fool of yourself to think of writing about Launcelot Panther. It was clever really."

"Could you bring the book home so we could read
about him?" Robin asked.

Gemma shook her head.

"Miss End confiscated it. I don't think it was clever
really, it was silly, but it was fun while it lasted."

Ann came in with the tea tray. She looked severely at
Lydia.

"And don't you think you can start anything like that.
Gemma is sorry now that she did."

Robin had finished laying the table. He looked at
Gemma thoughtfully.

"I don't believe you're sorry, Gemma. You aren't a
being-sorry sort of person, I mean not like we are."

Gemma thought that clever of Robin.

"No, I'm not sorry exactly. I think sometimes you have
to do things the wrong way to find out the right way. You

78

certainly do in pictures, often the director will say: 'Let's try it this way, Gemma, then if it doesn't work we'll try the other way.' "

Both Lydia and Robin kept their promise not to tell their parents about Gemma's trouble, but that did not mean they did not get to hear about it. The Launcelot Panther story was so ridiculous that Ursula, reading it out loud in the common room, had the teachers in hysterics.

"To think the leader was that little doe-faced innocent Gemma!" said the singing mistress. "I'll have her up in front where I can see her at the next lesson."

"So shall I," the games' mistress agreed.

But Ursula defended Gemma.

"You do as you like but I think she won't be any more trouble. She puzzles me, that child. You ought to have heard the way she said 'I do hate dullness.' And imagine, before she came here, she had a private governess."

A garbled version of what had happened in 1.E. began to filter through the school. Launcelot Panther was such an amusing name to have picked on and that his story had been written in class so unlikely. Naturally Philip was not the only member of The Steen to have a son or daughter at the Comprehensive. So one day, a fellow musician running into him, said:

"I hear you've got a future Ian Fleming in the family."

"How's that?" Philip asked.

"The story I heard from my boy is about your niece Gemma. She started her whole class writing an epic about a secret agent called Launcelot Panther. The joke seems to be the kids wrote it in class."

Philip laughed and passed the story off as of no importance. But at home he told Alice about it.

"I hear Gemma's been making herself conspicuous at school."

"I know," said Alice, "someone told me at the hospital, she's got a girl in Gemma's class. But I gather it's all over now."

Though it was all over, Philip, when he got a chance,

spoke to Gemma about it. He found her laying the table for supper.

"I heard from someone in the orchestra about Launcelot Panther."

Gemma flushed.

"Oh him! He's washed up. I'm working really hard now. I mean to be in 1.S. next term—or anyway soon."

"Good," said Philip. "I only mentioned it to point out that it's stupid to get yourself a bad name in a school. School teachers are like elephants—they never forget. You may think you've buried Launcelot Panther and anything else you got up to but you'd be wrong. You will find it is remembered and if there is trouble anywhere near you later on it will be you on whom suspicion will fall."

Gemma shrugged her shoulders.

"If I haven't done anything I shan't worry. Actually, because you know how it feels to be lower than a worm I don't mind telling you, while I was being bad it was fun. I only did it for kicks and because it made everybody in the class interested in me. Now I'm so good I couldn't be gooder. Did you see that picture about Pollyanna? Well, that's me. I'm all sunshine and light."

Philip laughed.

"Well, stick to it. And if you feel the need to break out again come and talk to me. Maybe together we could concoct something to boost your ego."

CHAPTER FIFTEEN: THE LETTER FROM AMERICA

ONE Saturday Lydia was invited by a school friend called Rose to a charity matinée. It was thrilling for her because the performers were all pupils of Headstone School of Drama and Stage Training. At the school, besides acting, the children were taught to dance both character and tap as well as ballet. Lydia was bored with the acting but fas-

...nated by the dancing, especially the ballets, because she could see how much better she was being taught in Miss Arrowhead's classes. She kept up a running commentary. "Terrible," she whispered to Rose. "Look at those knees!" "That girl dancing the solo was never properly on her pointes in those pirouettes." "Look at the way that one's tail sticks out."

Then a group of girls had come on to the stage who danced tap. For days after the matinée Lydia brooded on that tap dance and tried to do the steps. "If only I could learn that just for fun," she thought. "But Miss Arrowhead would have a fit if I suggested it. I bet if she thought I was learning tap she wouldn't teach me any more." But talking to herself didn't cure her of wanting to learn. In her head she heard the tap beat. "Oh, my goodness," she thought, "how I would love to make that shuffle pat pat noise."

Then one day Lydia had an idea and with Lydia to have an idea was to put it into immediate action. It was Sunday, in fact the idea had come to her during the sermon in church. After lunch she went to look for Gemma. It was a good day to get her on her own for Ann was spending the afternoon with a friend in the choir, Robin was in his bedroom playing with his model railway and her father and mother had gone to see someone's garden. Gemma was in the sitting-room writing a letter to her mother. Increasingly, as time passed, she found it difficult to find things to tell her mother which would interest her; that day she was really stuck so she was glad when Lydia came in.

"Hullo, Lydie! I thought you were practising your dancing."

"I was." Lydia sprawled across the table. "Have you thought any more about learning tap?"

"No. Polly says Miss Arrowhead knows where I can learn if I want to. But I rather like ballet. I'm never going to be any good but it's fun and I'm getting on all right."

Lydia looked earnestly at Gemma.

"I think you ought to learn. I don't mean give up Polly's class because that helps, but learn tap as well."

Gemma looked down at her half-finished letter.

"I don't get time to do much else. I mean with my homework and the banjo lessons and writing to Mummy and dancing, what time is there?"

Lydia pulled herself along the table closer to Gemma.

"You know that matinée I went to see? Well, some girls did tap at that. It was much the best thing in the matinée I thought, and so did everybody else for they clapped and clapped. There had been a lot of boring Shakespeare and the ballets were awful. This is how the leading dancer looked." Lydia got up and with her tail stuck out and her knees bent gave a cruel imitation of the star dancer.

Gemma laughed.

"I can't think how you can stand on your pointes in ordinary shoes."

"Miss Arrowhead would be mad if she saw me even doing it for fun. She says it will be more than time enough if I have blocked shoes when I'm eleven, and I'm not ten until next April."

"Why do you think I should learn tap?"

"Well, when you know how to I don't think tap's difficult. In the dance those girls did at the matinée they wore black top hats and sort of long-tailed black coats and, of course, tights, but the principal girl had a silver coat and I thought she looked like you. Wouldn't it be marvellous if you learned and got so good you danced at a concert! I mean you could at tap which you never could at ballet."

Gemma liked the picture of herself in a silver top hat and frock coat.

"Do you really think it's easy? Well, I suppose I could tell Polly I want to learn. It would have to be a Saturday afternoon class."

Lydia came back to the table.

"If you learn I'd like to come to your classes and watch what you do. It would be fun."

Gemma went back to her letter.

"O.K. I'll ask Polly." Then, to her mother she wrote: 'I am thinking of learning tap as well as ballet."

Polly, when asked about tap lessons, was very helpful. "The best place is the theatrical school. I don't know whether they have classes on Saturday afternoons but I expect they do. For they have a lot of pupils who only come on Saturdays. But it's no good joining now for they'll soon close down for the summer holidays. I should find out about it now and join in the autumn."

Gemma got Alice to write for a syllabus and when it came sure enough there was a beginners' class for character dancing and tap on Saturday afternoons.

"It seems to me it will leave you with very little free time," said Alice, "but if you want to learn I'll put your name down."

Lydia was very disappointed. When she wanted something she wanted it then and there, not months away, but there was nothing she could do about it, and she couldn't say too much for she had only told Gemma half the truth. She was not only going to watch her learn but meant her to teach her what she had learnt when she got home.

As it happened soon afterwards Gemma had other things to think about than tap dancing. The news came in a letter from her mother.

"I am afraid, darling, we may be parted for a long time. They are very pleased with the rushes of the film and my agent tells me he thinks I am to be offered a long-term contract. This could be for three or five years."

"Three or five years!" The words swam before Gemma's eyes. Why, in five years she would be sixteen, almost grown up. If she had heard a rumour of three or five years when her mother had left she thought she would probably have died. The letter had arrived at breakfast and, as always, she had put it in her pocket to read in break for there was no time in the rush to get off to school. When break came she took her milk to a deserted part of

83

the playground and so was reading the letter against a background of school break noises.

School! She had never considered staying that long in this school. She wasn't doing badly now she was working properly, but three or five years in Headstone Comprehensive! Could she bear it? "Not unless somehow I become a person," she thought, "not just a girl in 1.E."

Then she thought of the house. Funny—the little house in Trelawny Drive, which she had described to her mother as "awfully small and rather squalid", didn't seem particularly small any longer and not a bit squalid. "I suppose," she thought, "that's because I don't think about it at all except as just home."

Then she thought about the Robinsons. They were not a bit like she had thought they were. She had thought of them as dreadfully boring when she first came but they weren't now. Perhaps Ann was a bit prissy but she liked her and she was truly fond of Aunt Alice and Uncle Philip. But three or five years! It was a shatteringly long time.

Gemma went back to her letter.

"I thought this news would come as a shock to you and so I'm finishing with some nice news. I've told my lawyer to send you two hundred pounds. I want you to use it to take all the family away for a summer holiday as your guest. Of course you will want to talk it over with the cousins, but it's your treat so you must decide where you would like to go. I would think a small hotel would be the idea. Your poor Aunt Alice seems to lead a dog's life, it would do her good not to have to buy food or cook it."

Almost the three to five years were forgotten. A holiday for everyone! It wouldn't only do Aunt Alice good it would be marvellous for Uncle Philip. If it was by the sea it might help his hands. Should she find Ann and tell her now or should she wait and tell everybody together when Aunt Alice and Uncle Philip came home? No, better wait, it would be more exciting for them all that way.

he end of break bell began to ring. Gemma folded up
er mother's letter and put it in her pocket. Names of
laces ran through her mind. The Isle of Wight. Devon.
Cornwall. . . She couldn't wait to see everybody's face
vhen they heard her news. She would remember what
verybody said to tell Mummy. It never struck Gemma
hat if her mother could have been there to see the family's
eaction what would have interested her most was her
Gemma who, unlike the Gemma she had left behind, was
t that moment thinking only of other people and not at
ll about herself.

CHAPTER SIXTEEN: WHERE SHALL WE GO?

GEMMA waited until supper time to tell her news. The re-
eption was even more joyful than she had dreamed it
vould be.

"Two hundred pounds!" Alice gasped, her eyes shin-
ng. "How good of your mother, Gemma darling."

Philip at once began to make plans.

"If we could make the money last we could go for three
veeks. I've that much holiday due to me."

"I suppose it couldn't be Wales, could it?" Ann asked.
I've always wanted to go there and if I was lucky I might
e able to enter a singing competition at an eisteddfod."

Lydia bounced up and down in her excitement.

"What I'd like is a holiday like Rose went to last year.
t was a holiday camp. Everything free, she said, once
ou're staying there. And there are competitions for danc-
ng. I could enter because at a holiday camp Miss Arrow-
ead would never know."

"Couldn't we hire a motor launch?" Robin plead[ed]
"A boy at school had a holiday on one last year. I'd lov[e]
to live on a motor launch. And with an enormous sum
like two hundred pounds I should think we could hir[e]
dozens."

Philip held up a hand.

"Let's have a little less talk. The money is yours
Gemma. Where do you want to go?"

Gemma took her mother's letter out of her pocket.

"I'll read you what Mummy says. 'I've told my lawye[r]
to send you two hundred pounds. I want you to use it t[o]
take all the family away for a summer holiday as you[r]
guests.'" She skipped the bit that said it was her treat s[o]
she must decide where she wanted to go and changed th[e]
wording about Alice, just finishing up with: "'I woul[d]
think a small hotel would be the idea. It would do you[r]
Aunt Alice good not to buy food or cook it.'"

Alice leant back in her chair, already relaxing.

"Dear Rowena, how thoughtful of her! It will indee[d]
do me good not to have to shop or cook. Imagine three
whole weeks without thinking about meals!"

"I think where we can go for three weeks is going t[o]
depend on where we can get in," Philip said. "The sum
mer holidays are almost on us so I expect most places ar[e]
booked up."

"We might still get a motor launch," pleaded Robin

"Motor launches are out," Philip said. "On a moto[r]
launch Mum would still have to shop and cook."

"And the cooking would be more difficult than cook
ing at home," Alice pointed out. "I can't and won't coo[k]
in a galley."

"You must say where you would like to go," Phili[p]
told Gemma. "It will give us somewhere to start on."

Gemma's holidays with her mother had been eithe[r]
abroad to somewhere fashionable or to smart hotels o[n]
the south coast. She remembered a lot of dressing up an[d]
drinking orange juice while her mother talked to friend[s]

cocktails. She had never found holidays fun. But this ould be different.

"What would you think about Ireland? I've never been ere."

"The drawback to Ireland," said Philip, "is the fares. emember there are six of us. That means we have about 33 to spend on each of us."

"I tell you what," Ann suggested. "Why don't we all rite down a place we'd like to go to then you could draw ne out of a hat, Gemma?"

"Gemma better draw the lot out of the hat while she's t it," Philip said, "then we'll put them down in order, ecause, as it's so late, we may not get in at the first hoice."

Paper was torn up and they sat round chewing pencils nd thinking, except Lydia and Ann who knew what they anted. But at last everybody had written something. And ne papers were folded and put in Philip's hat.

"Quick, Gemma," said Robin. "The suspense is killing e."

Gemma shut her eyes and picked out the first paper. t was in Aunt Alice's handwriting and said "East- ourne."

The next out was Lydia's with "holiday camp" scrawled n it. Gemma's choice was third, she did not really care vhere they went but she thought Ann's choice sounded ice so she had put down "Wales". Ann's choice fol- owed Gemma's, she had written "North Wales." Then ame Robin's choice. He had backed Lydia since the notor launch was out and had written "Holiday camp y the sea". Philip's choice was last, he had written "Small otel by the sea".

Alice looked at the list.

"I don't really mind about Eastbourne," she said. "I hose it because it's not too expensive a fare. You can et all the way there by coach."

"You can to anywhere by coach if it comes to that,"

Philip reminded her. "But better stick to what we plan
You go to a travel agent first thing tomorrow, Alice, an
see if we can get in at Eastbourne."

Alice collected the slips of paper and put them in th
paper basket.

"As it happens I know a travel agent. Her husband wa
a patient in the hospital and we became quite friendl
when she visited him. She told me to come to her if I eve
wanted to go anywhere. At the time I laughed becaus
there was no chance of a holiday. But now she's just wha
we need."

The next day, when Alice opened the front door on he
return from the hospital, all the family rushed out to mee
her.

"Where are we going, Mum?" Robin shouted.

"Is it Eastbourne?" Lydia asked.

"Where is it, Mum? Don't hold out on us," An
pleaded.

"Yes, where are we going?" Gemma demanded.

Alice laughed.

"Give me time to get my breath. Anyway, I vote w
wait for Dad, he'll be in any minute now."

There were groans and cries of "Oh, must we!" "H
may be ages." But Alice was firm. "He won't be long
Who's got an atlas? You're going to need it."

Though it felt to the children like an hour it was actu
ally only ten minutes later that Philip came home. He wa
greeted with:

"Come on, Dad." "Mum won't say where we are goin
until you are here." "We've got an atlas to see where i
is."

Alice kissed Philip.

"It was lucky I knew Mrs. Amersham at the agency o
I don't think we'd have got in anywhere. She nearly ha
a fit when I asked where six people could go in Augus
and then she remembered something. Each year som
people take all the rooms on a farm and now they've ge

scarlet fever and can't go. But as they had booked they feel responsible for letting the farmer down so they asked Mrs. Amersham to find new tenants."

"But where, Mum?" Ann asked.

Her mother smiled.

"Not Wales I'm afraid but not far off. Open that map of south-west England." The map was opened. "Now find Devon." Alice bent over the map. "You see that place there in north Devon. Well, in the middle of where nothing is marked there is a farmhouse called Torworthy. It will be a bit of a squeeze for there are only two bedrooms and a slip room which will do for you, Robin. I'm afraid you three girls will have to share. But we can manage three weeks there, everything provided, well inside the £200. And Mrs. Amersham says there is wonderful bathing and Mrs. Yeo, the farmer's wife, is a splendid cook."

"Has Mrs. Amersham booked the rooms?" Philip asked.

"She sent a telegram. She knew Mrs. Yeo would be delighted because she said in the wire 'known to me personally'."

Devon! A county they had heard so much about and now they were going there. To the land of Devonshire cream. All other ideas, such as holiday camps, North Wales and motor launches, were forgotten. They were going to Devonshire and Devonshire was the place where they would most like to be.

CHAPTER SEVENTEEN: TORWORTHY

WHEN something is tremendously looked forward to it can, when it happens, be a disappointment. Before the holiday in Devon Alice had worried that this might happen for the family talked of nothing else. But as it turned out everything was perfect from start to finish.

First there was the coach journey and, though rather long, that was thrilling for there was so much to look at and, of course, the stops were superb, it was such fun eating snacks all day instead of proper meals.

The arrival was riotous. Mr. Yeo met them with his station wagon. He looked, the children decided, like an apple for his face was so red and shining. He was a very friendly man and all the way to Torworthy kept up a running flow of conversation, which they supposed was about the countryside, but on that first day they did not understand more than a word here and there. The children were in agonies trying to hold in their giggles as they heard Alice saying politely at intervals "Yes." "No." "Really!" clearly not following at all.

They were so tired that night that all the family practically fell asleep over the splendid supper Mrs. Yeo had waiting for them, which included—as did every meal at the farm—a great bowl of clotted cream. But the next morning they woke to find they were staying in what they then and always thought was the most beautiful place in the world.

Torworthy was inland but a path led down to a sandy cove. On each side of the path were steep banks which the whole family found enthralling. They were only used to ferns in pots but on that bank hart's-tongue ferns popped up naturally among ordinary plants like dandelions. Then the wild strawberries! These were the largest they had ever seen. Always afterwards those strawberries were remembered and fruit was judged by them. "These blackcurrants are almost as large as Torworthy's wild strawberries." "This year's holly has berries like Torworthy strawberries."

The weather was kind. All the morning the family rolled in and out of the sea. Then at lunch time they crawled home to one of Mrs. Yeo's superb mid-day meals, which she called "dinner". Afterwards even the children were glad of a rest and Alice and Philip, without any pretence, went to sleep.

Then there were walks to nearby villages. They did not all go to these. Robin found the farm was all the entertainment he needed and Lydia often stayed with him. Mrs. Yeo's children were grown up but she remembered what they liked to do and what the Stratford children, who should have been there if they had not got scarlet fever, liked to do so she allowed them to help feed the pigs and chickens and later shut them up for the night, and other interesting jobs which they could manage safely.

Perhaps because, even if miraculously Aunt Rowena sent another £200 next year, they could not come back to Torworthy for the Stratfords would be in their rooms, there seemed a sort of magic quality about the farm and the whole neighbourhood.

"I keep feeling that it isn't real," said Ann, "as if when we leave the Yeos and everybody on the farm will vanish as if they had never been."

Robin was proudly picking up what he thought was the Devonshire dialect, so when Ann said that he answered:

"It do be mortal beautiful, my dear soul."

Everybody laughed but Alice was quick to say:

"You must be careful not to talk like that when the Yeos are about or you might offend them."

"They know he does it and they don't mind," said Lydia. "I think they just think he's learning to speak properly."

"It is very catching," Philip pointed out. "Yesterday I was admiring the sunset and Mr. Yeo came along and said 'sweetly pretty it do be', and I found myself answering 'yes indeed it do be'. I'm sure he didn't notice."

In the sitting-room set aside for visitors there was a piano, an old upright badly in need of tuning. Nobody had used it for even Robin, who was always making up tunes on the one at home, had no time at Torworthy for he was out of doors. But one afternoon after her sleep Alice came down to find Philip playing. She caught her breath and stood in the doorway, her eyes wide with surprise for it was so long since he had touched a piano. Philip had heard her come in.

"My hands have got so much better with all this bathing I thought I'd try them out."

Alice was almost too pleased to speak.

"Oh darling! Are they really better? Oh, I'm so glad! "

Philip stopped playing and got up.

"Let's go for a walk. A holiday is a thinking time and I've done a lot of thinking since we've been here."

"Let's go down the sea path," said Alice. "I love that best of all."

Arm in arm they strolled down the lane. Silent at first then Philip said:

"I don't think—in fact I'm quite sure—my hands will never recover sufficiently to play with The Steen."

"Oh Philip! "

"Well, it's better to face facts," he said, "because it means I can make plans. That music library was always a temporary job and it's not for me. I must make music. So when we get home I'm going to resign and take on full

"Sweetly pretty it do be"

time teaching." Philip felt Alice was hugging his arm in pity. "Now I've made up my mind I don't mind as much as you would expect. Of course I care, I wouldn't be human if I didn't but, you know, such teaching as I've done I've always enjoyed."

"But you've only taken talented pupils."

"And that is all I shall teach now. I shall apply to join the staff at the Headstone music school, and I shall take a few private pupils."

Alice gazed unseeingly at a hart's-tongue fern on the bank. However brave Philip was about it she knew how he loved The Steen. Still, if he could be brave so could she.

"Someday you might have a music school of your own."

"That's possible. We must see how Robin develops, he might like to come in with me."

Nothing more was said about plans but having started to play the piano Philip played a little every evening. Soon, before bedtime, the whole family would stand round the piano singing. The first night they did this Mr. and Mrs. Yeo came in.

"Bless your lives, my dear souls," Mrs. Yeo said, sitting down on the horsehair sofa and pulling Mr. Yeo down beside her. "Do-ee go on now. Sweetly pretty it do be."

After that the Yeos came in every evening to listen and for their benefit the family added "Glorious Devon" to their repertoire of old favourites, such as "Annie Laurie", "Cherry ripe" and "Drink to me only". Each evening they finished with a hymn, often "Glory to Thee my God this night" sung in canon.

Gemma was not allowed to miss the singing.

"You'll soon know all the words," Philip encouraged her, and when they sang in canon he told her to sing with Alice, who had a strong if not very tuneful voice.

Gemma would sometimes think about herself when she was in bed. How odd that she was still the same person as she had been when she had lived in London. It seemed almost as if she ought to look different. She didn't mind a bit when the Yeos admired Ann and Robin's singing and Lydia's dancing. She didn't even mind when Mrs. Yeo, meaning to be kind, said: "We can't all be the clever ones I'll tell-ee, can we now?" "But deep inside I'm still me," she promised herself. "I'm still the person who was a star and will be a star again."

All too soon it was the last week. The last day. Then Mr. Yeo was driving them to catch the coach. All the family were unusually silent on the start of the coach drive home. Then Robin said:

"I think you were right, Ann, when you said it would all vanish when we went away. I believe, if we went back now, there would be no farm, no nothing."

Alice turned round to Gemma, who was in the seat behind her.

"It's been a glorious holiday and we've got you to thank for it, Gemma. I don't think Torworthy will ever vanish. Wherever else we may go it will have a place in our hearts for ever."

"And so, my dear soul, will the Yeos," said Robin.

CHAPTER EIGHTEEN: BACK AT SCHOOL

IT was the last day of the summer holidays. The family were collecting what they would need the next morning when Ann said:

"At the beginning of the summer holidays it seems as if they will go on for ever and ever. But at the end they go so fast you hardly seem to have had any holiday at all."

Alice, marking tapes on a pair of Robin's uniform shorts, looked up.

"What rubbish! You've had a glorious summer holiday, we all have. But there's been so much to do since we came back time has simply flown. Both you and Lydie had out-grown your winter uniforms and that meant shopping, and there has been something to buy for you, Gemma. And there's been all of your uniform to buy, Robin, and mark with these revolting tapes."

"And you've made me a new dancing tunic," Lydia reminded her, "and we've bought Gemma's shoes for tap."

"And we've left out the most important thing of all," Alice said. "In the short time we've been home Dad's given up The Steen and is starting on what really is a new life."

Philip was out seeing the principal of the music school so it was a good moment to ask questions.

"I will tell you what I was wondering," said Ann. "Did the directors of The Steen mind awfully Dad going? I mean, quite often he's stood in for the leader."

Alice folded the shorts she had finished marking.

"A fiddle player's hands are his tools, like voices are tools for singing and feet for dancing. I think they had been afraid Dad might have to retire so I suppose it was sort of expected."

Robin was indignant.

"They just let him go. Didn't they even say they were sorry?"

Alice looked amused.

"Of course they didn't just let him go. I wanted him to tell you what they said but he doesn't like talking about it."

"They might have given him a gold watch," said Lydia. "A girl at school's grandfather retired from a factory where he worked and he got a gold watch."

Alice sat up straight looking, Gemma thought, so proud she was like a queen.

"They said it was only a temporary good-bye. They said the orchestra and the town knew what they owed to Dad and at a later date they would say thank-you in an appropriate way."

"What's that mean?" asked Robin.

"A gold watch perhaps," Lydia suggested.

"I bet it means more than that," said Ann. "Will they give a party for him, Mum?"

"A party and a presentation." Alice smiled. "Goodness knows what form the presentation will take. Men have the funniest ideas about presents. It could be a clock, a canteen of silver, or if Dad's very unlucky, an inscribed silver salver, which I would have to keep clean and which would be no good at all, or of course, as Lydia says, it could be a gold watch."

"Poor Dad!" said Ann. "I bet he's miserable inside. I hope he soon gets lots of pupils so he's too busy to think."

Gemma remembered her talk with Uncle Philip. What was it he had said? "I daresay to you to be a first fiddle in The Steen seems unimportant, but to me it means a lot." And now he had stopped being a first fiddle for

97

ever. Without thinking she quoted something else he had said.

"I'm sure humility is a great virtue but I doubt if it brings out the best in most of us."

Alice looked at her.

"Oh, Gemma darling, whatever made you say that? Though it may be true of some people I promise you all it is not going to be true of Philip Robinson. He will never allow himself to feel humiliated and you may be sure the best of him will come out always."

"Poor Dad!" said Ann. "I suppose it's the rain but I feel very low. As if nothing nice would ever happen again. I mean school tomorrow, and you going back to the hospital, and Dad having to give up The Steen."

Alice got up.

"We're getting morbid. Let's make some toffee—always a good idea when things look black. But I like you saying nothing nice will ever happen again. Who has got a birthday in September?"

Ann was ashamed.

"Me." She hugged Alice. "You really are the nicest mother in the world."

The next morning the house was in a frenzy and both Gemma and Ann rather cross.

"I don't want any breakfast, Mum. Please don't make me eat," Ann protested.

"Truly anything would make me sick," said Gemma.

The truth was they were both nervous. Because it was the beginning of the school year they would move up. They would be class 2 now, or at least most of class 1 would. This meant new classrooms and a new teacher. There would be no Miss End to welcome them back, it would not even be a teacher they knew for last term's class 2 teacher had left to get married.

"You won't feel any better by going to school with empty insides," said Alice. "Leave the cereal and just eat your eggs and one piece of toast, and I'll give you a banana to eat at morning break."

"And isn't Miss Lydie Robinson to have a banana for morning break?" Lydia asked. "If you want to know I think I need it more than Ann and Gemma. I'm moving up too and for the first time I have to walk to school alone."

Her mother laughed.

"Certainly Miss Lydie Robinson shall have a banana too. But don't tell me any story about walking to school alone, you won't be alone, you've dozens of friends you'll pick up on the way."

Robin's choir school term did not start for two days and this was what Lydia thought tough.

"I may have friends but nobody likes being sent to school while their brother stays at home doing nothing."

"Oh dear!" said Gemma to Ann as they hurried off to school. "What will I do if I haven't moved up? I easily mightn't because I was only one term in form 1.E. Imagine if I'm left behind with that dumb Paul Perkins! I think I shall die of shame."

"Don't fuss," Ann advised. "I bet you'll move. In subjects such as English you're miles ahead of even 1.U. and you're good at French."

When they reached school Gemma found, as Ann had prophesied, that she had been worked up about nothing. She had been moved up. With perhaps the idea of encouraging the class to do well the three divisions of class 2 were known as T., O. and P. Gemma was now 2.P. But better even than being moved up was the fact that Gemma straight away took to her new teacher, Miss Pepper. She was young with red gold hair, so at once the class christened her nasturtium. But for Gemma she was an understandable person, for she had a vivid personality and so was much more like the sort of people she had been used to in her own world. From the beginning Miss Pepper set out to know each of her pupils, clearly she was never going to consider them in a lump. But even on that first morning Gemma could feel no one would get away with anything. "What luck," she thought, "I've given up being bad. I'd never have foxed her."

The first day of school brought exciting news for everybody. After break the whole school was marched into the assembly hall to be talked to by Mr. Stevens. Headstone, he told them, though it had a fine hospital, lacked kidney machines which could save lives. So it had been decided next year should be kidney machine year. It was hoped to raise £10,000. Naturally the school wanted to help.

"No doubt we'll hold a bazaar, as we've often done, and maybe some small functions, but I and my staff feel this calls for an all-out effort. So we are going to act a pageant. Headstone—rather the country round here—has a lot of history and that is what the pageant will be about. Now I'm going to ask my senior history teacher to tell you a little more about what is planned."

Mr. Seddon, senior history, looked a rather dried up man but it was said he came to life when he was teaching, and he certainly came to life that morning.

"I'm providing the history," he told the school, "and Mr. Weldon, senior English, is writing the pageant. Each class will perform one episode." He evidently saw some anxious faces for he added: "That doesn't mean you've got to learn a lot. The spoken parts will be taken by the drama section. The episodes are linked together by a boy and a girl who are on all through the pageant. It means you, each class of you, will be the people of the period you are given to act. In fact, what we shall want from all of you is enthusiasm, time and a bit of help from your mothers with the clothes, and probably your Dads, too, where armour is needed. It is proposed the pageant shall be acted in the park each evening in a week in June."

Of course news like that set the school buzzing. The boys, who had not been very enthusiastic when Mr. Stevens was talking, felt quite differently when Mr. Seddon spoke about armour, and they went back to their classrooms with the clash of steel ringing in their ears.

The talk had a strong effect upon Gemma. In films, when there were street scenes or places like a church where a lot of people were needed, extras were engaged. It was quite hard, she had been told, to get on to the list of extras. How much they were paid and how they were engaged was fixed by Union laws. But on the set they were people apart, they never had, outside the action of the picture, anything to do with the principal players and their stand-ins. Clearly, from what Mr. Seddon had said, what each school class would be was in effect extras, and that was something Gemma had no intention of being. Her professional pride couldn't take it. However, she had been at school long enough to know that to refuse to take part in a school thing just wasn't done. Casually on the way home, as if it had no interest for her, Gemma questioned Ann.

"What is the drama group that Mr. Seddon talked about?"

"They do plays," said Ann vaguely. "They meet after school."

"But I mean how do they join?"

"They go and ask to, I think they have to read parts and recite things to see if they are any good." Ann shot a quick look at Gemma. "It's awfully difficult to join. I mean they have plenty of members already, and nobody joins under class 3 and then they're lucky if they get in."

"I see," said Gemma and changed the subject. But to herself she said: "The drama group have a surprise coming. Someone is going to join who is only in class 2.P. Drama group, though you'll never know it, Gemma Bow is coming."

CHAPTER NINETEEN: BIRTHDAY PARTY

THE whole family was so busy that none of them had much time to notice what anybody else was up to.

Alice, on top of her hospital work, had been roped in to serve on a committee which was organising a concert to help raise the ten thousand pounds.

"Luckily it's in the autumn," she told the children, "so your pageant will be over and you can help me."

Philip was surprised at the amount of work which came to him. There seemed, both at the music school and privately, quite a number of talented pupils who were needing expert teaching. He enjoyed the work and it helped heal the wound made in him when he gave up The Steen. As well, though he was not supposed to know about it, he could not help hearing rumours of a subscription list for a parting present for him. It was to be given him at a dinner at Christmas.

Ann found that the school choir had a lot of music to prepare for the pageant. Already, though the pageant would not take place until June, there was an extra choir practice each week. This, on top of her church choir work, kept her very busy.

Gemma was now as busy as any member of the family, especially on Saturdays. First, there was her dancing class with Polly. Then she had to rush home for her lesson with Ted. She was getting on nicely with the banjo. That term Ted promoted her from just learning fingering and basic chords to accompanying herself in a song. He decided that as she had not much voice something very simple was needed. He chose "There was a lady loved a swine.". Then immediately after lunch Gemma had to rush off clutching her tap shoes to the drama school for her tap dancing lesson. Lydia always came with her to this and, something Gemma had not reckoned on, insisted on being shown any new step directly they got home. But this she soon realised was rather lucky because, even just watching, Lydia missed nothing and, though she had no proper shoes for tap dancing, could often show Gemma how a step should be danced.

To Lydia dancing wasn't work, if it had been she would have been a very overworked nine-year old. There were three lessons a week now with Miss Arrowhead as well as her Saturday morning class. There was Gemma's tap class, which Lydia took very seriously, and there was at least half an hour's practise each day.

Robin was enchanted with the choir school but he had to work hard. All the new boys had a probationary period while they learnt the church music and some of the anthems. During this period they came to church with the choir wearing the scarlet cassock and white frilled collar, but they were not allowed to sing a note, and they were conspicuous as new boys because they did not wear surplices. Robin thought this infra dig so he worked really hard not only at choir practice but at home. His great hobby, when he was not making up tunes on the piano, was what he called "swirling". This meant taking an old tune and what his father called "messing it up", but he gave up both tune making and swirling while he was mastering the church music. To his father, who helped him in the evening, he would say daily:

"I'm going to be the quickest choir boy they've ever had to wear a surplice."

Busy though they all were everything was given up on the last Saturday evening of the month for Ann's birthday. The actual birthday had been the previous Tuesday but there was no time to keep it then so, except for presents, it was moved to Saturday. There had been endless discussions as to how the birthday should be celebrated. In the end it was decided there would be an evening party with games and, because it was Ann's party and most of the guests were friends from the choir, there would be singing.

It was surprising how many people squeezed into the little house and, having squeezed in, how room was found for competitions. There were ten of these and each scored marks and at the end there were prizes. Then Alice provided a really magnificent fork supper, finishing with a huge pink and white birthday cake with twelve candles on it.

After supper Philip sat down at the piano and there was singing. Not family singing like they had sung at Torworthy but lovely trained choir singing. After that there were solos, not just from Ann but from most of the guests, and Robin, to much applause, sang "Cherry ripe". Then one of the guests turned to Lydia.

"Could you dance, Lydie?"

Lydia looked round.

"If you all squeeze against the wall I could."

"Oh Lydie," said Alice, "I thought you weren't supposed to dance in public."

"This isn't public, it's home," Lydia retorted. "Dad, would you play 'The Irish washerwoman'?"

It was even lovelier, Lydia thought, than when she had danced the same jig for Miss Arrowhead and the big girls. Everybody squeezed back and made room, the carpet was rolled up so she had, as it were, a little stage on which she was dancing, truly properly dancing.

There was a real storm of applause when the dance came to an end. And everybody showered praise on Lydia. Then somebody said to Gemma:

"Don't you do anything?"

Philip came, as he thought, to Gemma's rescue.

"There was a lady loved a swine"

"She hasn't a show piece yet, have you, Gemma? How about another song?"

Gemma surprised the family.

"If you don't mind my not having a grand singing voice like you all have I can sing to my own accompaniment on the banjo."

The banjo was fetched and when it was tuned Gemma sat down on the music stool Philip had vacated. She was wearing a new blue frock her mother had sent her from Hollywood. It suited her perfectly and knowing this gave her confidence. She struck a chord and then softly began to sing:

"There was a lady loved a swine,
   'Honey!' said she;
'I'll build thee a silver sty,
   Honey!' said she.

'Pig-hog wilt thou be mine?'
   'Hunc!' said he.
'And in it thou shalt lie!'
   'Hunc!' said he.

'Pinned with a silver pin,
   Honey!' said she;
'That thou mayest go out and in.'
   'Hunc!' said he.

'Will thou have me now,
   Honey?' said she;
'Speak, or my heart will break,'
   'Hunc!' said he."

Gemma sang very simply, using all her wistful charm for the lady, but a good loud pig noise for the pig. Everybody was charmed and the family incredulous.

"Goodness, Gemma!" said Ann. "I never knew you were getting on as well as that."

"It's a good song," Robin stated. "I'd like to swirl it for you."

"At next year's party," Lydia announced, "Gemma will be able to do a tap dance."

Presently Philip went back to the piano and there was more singing until Alice served cold drinks and cake and the party was over.

"Bed all of you," said Alice when everybody had gone. "Dad and I will tidy up."

When the children had gone to bed Philip and Alice looked at each other.

"Well," said Alice, "I suppose when you are used to appearing in public you do it naturally all your life. I don't think anybody noticed how professional Gemma was. Do you?"

"Probably not," Philip agreed. "From their point of view she hasn't much of a singing voice. It was the way she put the song over that was so noticeable. If she wants to remain Gemma Robinson she better not sing to her banjo in public."

"Come to that, Ann sang beautifully and so did Robin, and you must say Lydie danced like an angel."

"Our lot are quite talented but amateurs—very obvious amateurs. Now Gemma isn't talented, I mean not at what she was doing, yet it was very noticeable to me that she did not belong to the amateur world."

Alice straightened the carpet.

"If she wants to appear in public I don't see how we can stop her."

"We can't. All I'm saying is that if she does, sooner or later someone will spot that she is a professional. You wait and see."

CHAPTER TWENTY: THE DRAMA GROUP

THE next week Gemma tackled Miss Pepper about the drama group. She stayed behind after school to ask her advice.

"How do I join the drama group? My cousin Ann in 2.T. says you can't until you are in class 3, but I should think that must be wrong, wouldn't you?"

"What makes you want to join?" Miss Pepper asked. "Have you done any acting?"

Gemma had worked out an answer to that.

"In London I did a lot. My mother was keen so when a child was wanted they used me."

Miss Pepper always gave straight answers.

"As I'm new here I have not had time to find out about the outside school hours goings-on, but I will find out and I'll let you know."

The next day when she went into the common room for coffee break Miss Pepper went to Ursula End.

"Your ex-pupil Gemma Robinson asked me yesterday about the drama group. Is it true you can't join it until you are in class 3?"

There were several play producers in the school but Ursula led Miss Pepper to a Miss Jenkins, a fair rather intense-looking young woman who specialised in drama though she taught English.

"Miss Pepper has inherited that pupil of mine, Gemma Robinson, who invented Launcelot Panther. She wants to join the drama group."

"How old is she?"

"Eleven," said Miss Pepper.

Miss Jenkins shook her head.

"Then I'm afraid the answer is 'no'. Eleven is a bit young, you see sometimes, especially when we are rehearsing a play, we have to keep the cast on late, so it's been our policy not to use the younger pupils."

"Her cousin Ann is about the same age," Ursula pointed out, "and she sings in the choir so she has to stay late on occasion."

"I remember about Ann," Miss Jenkins said. "But an exception was made for her because she has got an unusually good voice."

"Gemma may be an unusually good actress," Miss Pepper retorted. "She seems to have done quite a bit of it in London."

"Where?" Miss Jenkins asked.

Miss Pepper shrugged her shoulders.

"I don't know, she just said her mother was keen so when a child was wanted she was used."

"I can imagine!" said Miss Jenkins. "Full of mannerisms which we've no time to cure. Tell Gemma to ask again next year when we'll see if we can find room for her."

Gemma, when she was told to apply next year, was furious. "If the drama group knew who they were turning down they'd kill themselves," she told herself. "Silly fools! Who wants to be in the drama group anyway? Lot of amateurs."

Gemma could talk to herself as much as she liked but she could not talk herself out of wanting to join the drama group. She wanted to join even more when she heard what class 2 were doing in the pageant. Miss Pepper told them about it.

"In old Headstone village, some of which, as you know, is still standing, there was an early charity school. It was built out of money left by a good old man who had helped Lord Shaftesbury work on the bill which finally made it illegal to employ boys as chimney sweeps. The school was for boys and girls, who were to be taught to read, write, the use of the globe and Holy Scripture."

There were groans from the boys at this news. They had hoped to be knights in armour or, better still, highwaymen, for some famous highwaymen were said to have worked on the old coach road which was near Headstone. But most of the girls were pleased. They fancied themselves as Victorian school children.

To Gemma it was shocking news. The charity school sounded all too like her film about an orphanage. There a crowd of extra children had been engaged; from her lofty position as star of the picture she had watched them from afar. It was really beyond bearing that she would now be one of the crowd while people from the drama group swanked about acting whatever parts there were. She couldn't—she wouldn't—stand for it. There were limits to what she could endure.

Because he had been sympathetic before Gemma took her troubles to her uncle. She managed to catch him alone on the next Sunday afternoon. He was reading a paper in the sitting-room but he put it down when she came in.

"Hullo, Gemma!"

Gemma sat on the arm of his chair and poured out her troubles.

"I don't think I'd have minded so much," she finished, "but you do see how like that scene will be to my picture when I was an orphan."

Philip nodded.

"I can see the connection. But I'm glad the authors of the pageant have remembered The Red Cloak School, which was what it was called instead of its proper name The Charles Prince Charity School. It was called that because the girls were given red cloaks and the boys red scarves. It was sad the school disappeared when education became compulsory."

"But that makes it worse," said Gemma. "If we all wear

red cloaks we'll all look exactly alike. I'd loathe that."

Philip spoke firmly.

"If you take my advice, Gemma, you'll just accept your lot. Honestly I wouldn't advise pushing yourself forward, not if you want to remain Gemma Robinson that is."

Gemma was annoyed that Uncle Philip could be so dense.

"I don't want a grand part. All I want is not to be a sort of extra."

"I can see how you feel and why you feel like it but you've had your answer, and you can't join the drama group until next year."

"You don't join the choir until you are in class 3 but Ann has."

"I suppose there are exceptions, but I wouldn't ask to be one if I were you."

"Well, I'm going to," said Gemma. "So what I want to know is, if you were me how would you get in?"

Philip sighed.

"I don't approve but if you must try I can't stop you. There is a good rule in life which is when you want something go to the top. In your case that is your headmaster, Mr. Stevens. I suppose he could get you into the drama group if he wanted to."

Gemma stared at her uncle.

"Mr. Stevens! He doesn't know I exist. Nobody speaks to Mr. Stevens unless they are sent to sit in his black chair as a punishment. I don't think I could ask him."

"Good," said Philip, "for I think you may make a mistake if you do. A professional is a professional, Gemma, and an amateur is an amateur. They look at things from an entirely different angle. If you get into that drama group you'll see what I mean."

Gemma thought and thought about going to see Mr. Stevens. The more she thought about it the more impossible it seemed. How did a person call on him? Could you just go to his door and knock? And if you did knock and

'*Then, white with terror, she sat down in the punishment chair*'

he said "Come in" what did you say? "I'm Gemma Robinson in class 2.P. And please I want you to say I am to join the drama group." It was obvious that wouldn't work. Mr. Stevens would probably say he didn't talk to anyone who had not an appointment.

In the middle of the following week Gemma found her answer. It was a frightening answer but it was a certain way of getting Mr. Stevens to speak to her. During morning break, shaking with fright but with her chin up, she marched down one corridor and up another until she came to the centre of the school. Then, white with terror. she sat down in the black punishment chair.

Ann had said that when Mr. Stevens came out of his office if he found anyone in his chair he lectured them in public. It hadn't sounded very awful when Ann was telling about it, but when you were actually sitting in the chair it was worse, far worse, than she had said it would be. No wonder a boy in 3.Y. had nearly cried. So many people passed and they stared and looked down their noses. Besides, Ann hadn't said how long you had to sit and be stared at. The bell for the end of break went and still Mr. Stevens hadn't come. The next class would be starting soon. What was she going to say to Miss Pepper about being late? The corridor was empty now, everybody had gone to their classrooms. Still the door of Mr. Stevens' room was shut. Then, from the wrong direction. there were footsteps. Looking up Gemma saw Mr. Stevens coming down the corridor. He had, though she did not know it, taken morning coffee with his staff. He stopped in front of Gemma and put on the official glare he kept for those sent to his chair.

"What is your name?"

"Gemma Robinson."

"What class are you in?"

"2.P."

Mr. Stevens was surprised but he managed to hide it. He had just been talking to Miss Pepper and she had said nothing about having sent a pupil to him although it was unusual to send children in the lower classes to the chair. He tried another of his glares while he wondered what crime this little white-socked girl could possibly have committed. But before he could ask Gemma explained.

"I haven't done anything. But I wanted to ask you something and this was the only way I could think of which would make you talk to me."

Mr. Stevens was amazed for he knew his chair was dreaded throughout the school.

"Rather a drastic means, wasn't it?"

"I suppose so but you don't usually talk to any of us, do you, especially not as low as 2.P.?"

Mr. Stevens did not mean to be inaccessible but with a thousand pupils he had to be.

"You are sure Miss Pepper didn't send you?"

"Oh, I promise. I came on my own. She'd be very surprised if she saw me here."

"All right." Mr. Stevens opened his study door. "Come in."

It was rather a nice room with a green carpet and green curtains, and there was a bowl of chrysanthemums on the desk. Mr. Stevens had a chair behind his desk, he pointed to another on the other side.

"Sit there. What did you say your name was?"

"Gemma. Gemma Robinson."

Mr. Stevens suddenly remembered. This was the child who had invented Launcelot Panther. However, he did not mention that.

"Your sister sings."

"No, she's my cousin, her name is Ann."

"Well, Gemma, what did you want to see me about so desperately that you came and sat in the punishment chair?"

Gemma had planned what to say, but now she was facing Mr. Stevens it all went out of her head.

"It's this pageant. I can't explain exactly but I've done
114

a lot of acting. So I don't just want to be an extra in it. I want to join the drama group."

"An extra?"

"Yes, you know, one of the crowd. Class 2 are being that charity school. Well, I'd have to wear a red cloak and look just like everyone else and I'd hate that."

Mr. Stevens, as he listened to Gemma's clear-dictioned English, had an odd feeling that he had heard that voice before. But he couldn't have. If so, where?

"When did you join the school?"

"Last term when I came to live with the cousins."

Information about Ann was coming back to him.

"Your uncle played with The Steen, didn't he?"

"That's right. I asked him who I should ask about the drama group. He said I should go to the top so I came to you."

Mr. Stevens was not sure of the arrangements about joining the various groups.

"We make rather a feature of drama in this school. There is a Miss Jenkins you could ask, she's very keen."

"It's no good my asking her," Gemma explained. "Miss Pepper asked her and she said I should try next year. But next year is no good to me, I want to join now."

Gemma, without realising, had used an almost imperious tone. Mr. Stevens was amused. "This little girl," he thought, "certainly has something to her."

"You run along," he said, "or you'll be in trouble for missing your lesson, you can explain you were with me. When I see Miss Jenkins I'll have a word with her about you."

CHAPTER TWENTY-ONE: THE AUDITION

MR. STEVENS did not forget his promise to Gemma. That very afternoon after school he sent a message to Miss Jenkins saying he would like to see her. It was not his custom to interfere with the way the groups were run, so he tried to be tactful.

"I had a visit from a little girl in form 2.P. this morning. She wants to join the drama group. She asked me to use my influence to get her in. Is there any reason why she should not join?"

Miss Jenkins was so amazed that a child in one of the lowest classes should approach the headmaster that she could not at first think of a suitable answer.

"No, not really I suppose. We don't use the small ones much in our productions, as you know, for there is the difficulty about keeping them late."

"I gather that won't matter in this case. There is a cousin of the same age singing in the school choir."

Her talk with Miss Pepper came back to Miss Jenkins.

"Oh! I think I know who you mean. Is the child called Robinson?"

"That's right. Gemma Robinson. It seems she's done some acting in London. I noticed her voice, she has a delightful speaking voice."

Miss Jenkins thought she was the one to decide if a child had a good speaking voice or not.

"The trouble of course with the drama group is that what we are always short of is boys. We don't need any more girls."

Mr. Stevens looked sympathetic.

"I leave it entirely to you but I would be glad, as she has approached me, if you would see the child."

Miss Jenkins, since that was an order, replied politely "Of course, Mr. Stevens," but inside she was boiling. As she scurried off to a drama reading she muttered to herself: "He's no right to interfere. As if we who take the outside groups had not enough work already without troubling us to see every little girl who fancies herself as an actress."

However, she could not disregard Mr. Stevens' wishes, so a day or two later she went up to Miss Pepper at coffee break.

"That child in your class. Gemma Robinson. Will you send her to me in break tomorrow morning. I'll see her in my classroom."

Gemma went home in a great state of excitement, but she had to keep her news to herself for there was no one she could tell. Uncle Philip had advised her not to try and join the drama group. Ann would be terribly shocked if she knew how she had made Mr. Stevens talk to her. She could, of course, tell Lydia but she didn't want to do that in case Miss Jenkins would not let her join.

"If only I need not wear uniform," she thought. "I look so much nicer in my own clothes. But one thing I can do, I can take these beastly ribbons off my hair. I can easily tie it back before I go to my class."

The next morning directly the bell rang for break Gemma ran to Miss Jenkins' classroom but, even though she had run, Miss Jenkins had the look of somebody who has been kept waiting. She glanced at a bit of paper and said, as if there were dozens of names on it:

"Are you Gemma Robinson?"

"Yes."

Miss Jenkins looked at Gemma. Actually she was surprised by her. Unwillingly she had to admit to herself she was a pretty child. But what she said was:

"Your hair should be tied back." Then, before Gemma could answer: "Can you recite something?"

Whatever faults Miss Court had as a governess she had taught Gemma to appreciate English. Both prose and poetry.

"Would you like poetry or Shakespeare?" Gemma asked. "Or I could do some modern prose."

"Shakespeare."

Gemma moved away from her and acted Titania's quarrelling speech with Oberon. She went right through the speech beginning "These are the forgeries of jealousy".

Miss Jenkins was amazed. Who was this child who spoke Shakespeare's words as if she understood them? Had a speaking voice without a trace of accent? She had even been taught to breathe. At last she said:

"Now let me hear some verse."

Gemma had planned beforehand what she would recite if verse was asked for. It had been one of Miss Court's favourites. She said clearly: "Home-thoughts, from Abroad by Robert Browning":

"O to be in England
Now that April's there,
And whoever wakes in England
Sees, some morning, unaware,
That the lowest boughs and the brushwood sheaf
Round the elm-tree bole are in tiny leaf,
While the chaffinch sings on the orchard bough
In England—now!

And after April, when May follows,
And the whitethroat builds, and all the swallows!
Hark, where my blossom'd pear-tree in the hedge
Leans to the field and scatters on the clover
Blossoms and dewdrops—at the bent spray's edge—
That's the wise thrush; he sings each song twice over,

118

Lest you should think he never could recapture
The first fine careless rapture!
And though the fields look rough with hoary dew,
All will be gay when noontide wakes anew
The buttercups, the little children's dower
—Far brighter than this gaudy melon-flower!"

When Gemma finished speaking Miss Jenkins sat quite
still for a moment. Then she asked:

"Who taught you?"

"My governess, Miss Court. You see, she was crazy on
poetry. As a matter of fact I quite like it."

Miss Jenkins wanted to know much more. Who had
taught Gemma to think what she was saying? Who had
taught her to stand naturally? Who had kept her voice
so free of accent? But there was no time for that now.

"You can join the drama group. But I'm afraid you'll
find it dull. We are working on one of the old Christmas
morality plays at the moment and there is nothing for you
in it. After Christmas work will start on the pageant—
we haven't thought about casting that yet. If I were you
I should join next term."

But Gemma, having got her foot in, was not taking it
out.

"Thank you," she said, "but I should like to join now."

It was a good thing for Gemma that she was so busy for
on the day after her talk with Miss Jenkins the letter came
for her from her mother about the future. It was a radi-
antly happy letter. She had signed a contract with her film
company, it was for five years.

Gemma, trying to pretend she did not mind, told the
family about her letter.

"I'm afraid I've bad news for you all. My mother has
signed that contract. It looks as if you're stuck with me
for five years."

Alice felt a lump in her throat for Gemma was not de-
ceiving her. "Poor child!" she thought. "Rowena really

is a callous mother. She must know the child adores her."
To Gemma she said:

"I've heard from your mother too. As you know, we love having you but we can't expect to keep you all the time. Perhaps your mother will be back between pictures and later on, when you are older, you can go out to stay with her."

"I'm glad you're staying," said Robin. "We've got used to you being here, and I'm swirling some songs for your banjo."

Lydia thought about the tap dancing.

"I'm glad too."

They were at supper. Ann was sitting beside Gemma. She didn't say anything but she gave her hand a squeeze under the table. It was meant to say "I'm sorry for you but glad for us," but Gemma was not in the mood for hand-squeezing so she pulled it away. She was not going to tell any of them but not once in her letter had her mother said anything about missing her. In fact it seemed to her clear that she was glad to be rid of her. "Oh well, if that was how Mummy felt," she told herself, "I won't bother about her any more. Somehow, some way I'll make my own life and when Mummy comes home and wants me back she won't get me."

CHAPTER TWENTY-TWO: CHRISTMAS

IT was Christmas. Gemma had never had a family Christmas. When she had lived with her mother Christmas day had been a going-out sort of day. Usually they lunched at a restaurant and in the evening they dined with friends. In the days when she had a Nannie she had hung up a stocking which had been filled, but that had come to an end when Miss Court took over for she went to relations for Christmas. Gemma had, of course, had presents, piles of them, most of them expensive and all beautifully wrapped. Both at home and wherever she was taken there were Christmas trees. Many years she had worked over Christmas and only had perhaps two days off. Working over Christmas had given Gemma the nicest Christmasses she had known for there was always a party for the children of the staff to which she was invited.

Early in December Gemma discovered that Christmas in Trelawny Drive was something she knew nothing about. Christmas cards came first; these the children made at home, each card being designed for whoever was to receive it. Then there was present buying. To her cousins this meant very careful spending of their money. Each of them seemed to know exactly what everybody else wanted, the trouble was to buy it with the money they had saved. To Gemma, well provided with pocket money, finances were no problem, but what did everybody want? It was so difficult to find out.

"Oh dear, do help me," Gemma begged Ann. "I do

want to give everybody things they need but how do I find out?"

They were in bed and the lights were out so Gemma could not see how puzzled Ann looked.

"But you must know. You've only got to listen and you'll hear what everybody wants. Then all you have to do is to find out that nobody else is giving it."

"But couldn't you help?" Gemma pleaded.

Ann would not do that. To her one of the nicest things about Christmas was finding out what people really wanted. Gemma had as much chance to learn as anybody.

"I was thinking I'd give Lydie a new case for her dancing things. Hers is very old."

"That'll be nice," said Ann.

Gemma sat up in bed.

"You don't think she wants that?"

"I know something she wants far more."

"What?"

"I'll give you a hint," said Ann. "You are the one person who does know how badly she wants these. Well, I do but not as well as you do."

"These." Gemma stared into the night. Something that she was the one person who knew about. What did she and Lydie do together? Almost nothing. That meant two of whatever it was. Then it came to her.

"Oh Ann! You mean tap shoes."

Ann turned over and settled herself down to sleep.

"I knew you'd guess. Well, everybody is like that. If you watch and listen you'll find out."

So Gemma watched and listened and finally shopped.

"My goodness!" she told Ann. "I do hope everybody will be pleased. And none of you are choosing what I've chosen."

"I should think you're pretty safe," said Ann. "What you spend and we spend will be quite different."

Nearer Christmas there were decorations. Some made at home and some bought, and all put away until the first day of the holidays, which was by tradition decorating day.

"But the grandest moment," Lydia told Gemma, "is when the tree comes. Mum and Dad decorate it after we're in bed on Christmas Eve and when we come down on Christmas morning there it is all lit up."

"And we put our presents under it," said Robin.

Christmas was also celebrated at school. There was a carol service at which Ann sang two solos. There was the old morality acted by the drama group. Gemma, with all the rest of the group who were not acting or being stage hands, sold programmes for this. Both these entertainments were open to the public and the money collected went towards buying a dog for a blind person. As well there was a school party at which the music for dancing was provided by the various school pop groups. This was quite an evening with crackers and refreshment.

That Christmas there was an added excitement. This was the dinner and presentation to Philip. It was to happen in the first week in January. It was to be quite a big dinner in Headstone's largest hotel.

"Such a mercy it's a men only affair," said Alice, "for I've nothing in the way of an evening dress to wear, and it would be such a waste to buy one for I should never put it on again."

"I think it's awfully mean it's men only," said Lydia. "I don't mind telling you Miss Lydie Robinson was looking forward to seeing her father get a present."

Gemma could not see how Christmas was going to be much fun for Ann and Robin. Both had to be in church by 9.30 and they sang again at 11 a.m. But when she said this Ann contradicted her.

"Oh, it's gorgeous to process into the church on Christmas day," said Ann. "Everything is crimson and white with great bowls of lilies on the altar and masses of holly everywhere, and, of course, a Christmas tree and a crib. We come in singing 'O come, all ye faithful'."

"We sing that too," said Robin, "but we call it 'Adaste, fideles'."

Ann laughed.

"Hark at somebody who has only been allowed to wear a surplice for six weeks."

Robin did not care.

"Even then I got mine quicker than any other boy in the choir. And we do call it 'Adaste, fideles'."

For Gemma Christmas began when her mother's parcel arrived from America. She might have told herself she was not going to bother about Mummy any more but, of course, it was not true, she still missed her terribly, though it was true that she had accepted she had to live her life without her—or at least for the next five years she had to.

Nothing could be private in the little house in Trelawny Drive, now more crowded than usual with parcels all over the place and the undecorated Christmas tree in the hall. So when the enormous crate arrived, though it was marked "Christmas", she unpacked it in the hall with the cousins sitting on the stairs to watch her do it. But unpacking it did not mean they found out what was in the parcels for inside everything was gift wrapped in the most elegant American style. There was a gold-wrapped box for Ann and a pink one for Lydia. A dark blue one for Robin. Alice's parcel, which was soft, was wrapped in silver with blue bows and twinkling silver rosettes.

"Oh goodness! " sighed Lydia. "Won't Mum be thrilled when she gets in and sees that!"

For Philip there was a small green parcel with green bows. Then, from the bottom of the box, came Gemma's parcels. All the colours of the rainbow trimmed with sprays of holly and mistletoe and tiny animals and dolls.

"Goodness! " said Ann. "Aunt Rowena is a gorgeous parcel packer."

Gemma, her arms full of parcels, only smiled. She was not going to spoil Ann's picture of Mummy by telling her all the parcels had been what the shops called "Gift wrapped".

Christmas day, when it arrived, was just as the cousins had said it would be. It had a sort of shimmer of happiness over it from waking up to going to bed. Alice and Philip had been to church at midnight but they managed to wake up when very early all the children clambered on to their bed to open their stockings. Although Gemma had opened a stocking before it had been alone except for Nannie, so it was not fun like it was with the cousins. Christmas stockings, she discovered, had a special smell made up of tangarines, oranges, chocolate and a queer special smell, which she decided must be Christmas smell.

When they came down for breakfast, just as the cousins had promised, there was the Christmas tree lit and decorated.

"It's the most beautiful tree we ever had," said Lydia.

Ann examined the ornaments for old friends.

"Here's the angel with the trumpet, and here is my most favourite—this little silver horse with the roses on him."

"Let's get the parcels," Robin shouted. "A tree isn't properly a tree until the parcels are under it."

By nine o'clock Ann and Robin had gone. Gemma and Lydia helped clear and wash up breakfast and tidy the rooms. Then it was time for church. Alice could not go because she had the lunch to cook though, as everybody's nose told them, the turkey had been cooking since before breakfast.

It was nice walking to church with Uncle Philip calling out "Happy Christmas" to the passers-by. The church, when they got there, was just as Ann had promised—a glory of crimson and white with an enormous tree covered in toys for children in hospital, and a lovely crib with a star blazing over it.

Ann, Gemma thought, looked very nice when she processed in with the choir. In that church the girls wore blue three-cornered caps and blue gowns, and at their necks

125

small white frills. But Ann's great moment came when, during the collection, she sang a solo carol "Sweet was the song the Virgin sang", the choir joining in at the "Lula, Lula" refrain.

Alice had made the table look very pretty. There were red candles, a decoration of holly and mistletoe and red and white crackers and the Christmas food was perfect. However, even the best food can't be sat over too long when the parcels are waiting outside to be unpacked.

Gemma always remembered that first Christmas with the cousins. She had never before taken so much trouble to give the right presents. She was really trembling with excitement when she watched Alice undo her parcel. But she need not have worried, she had been right in what was wanted.

"Oh Gemma! " said Alice as she hugged her. "An electric mixer! My darling child, I have wanted one for years."

It was the same with the rest of the family. Lydia, though she smuggled the box out of sight, was enchanted.

"Oh Gemma! You absolute angel! I can't wait to put them on."

Ann had once told Gemma that for concerts her mother lent her a necklace because Gemma's cast-off dress seemed to need it. So Gemma, choosing something she would like herself, gave Ann a necklace. It was not valuable but very pretty. Ann was so pleased Gemma was quite embarrassed.

"It's perfect. It's the prettiest necklace I've ever seen."

Gemma hoped both Philip and Robin were equally pleased with their presents but they were less demonstrative.

Robin, putting his fountain pen in his pocket, said:

"Oh good, I wanted that. Thanks awfully, Gemma."

Philip smiled as he opened a new book about a violinist called Joachim.

"Thank you, Gemma. I wanted to read that."

Rowena managed to please the younger members of the family. Ann and Lydia were delighted with matching knitted caps, scarves and gloves. Robin was charmed with a new type of airgun. But poor Alice sighed as she looked at her smart rather elaborately trimmed bed jacket; when did Rowena think a woman with four children to see off to school wore a garment like that? Philip took one look at the very fancy cuff-links in his parcel and hurriedly put them in his pocket, no one must see them for he knew he would never wear them.

Gemma's presents were all beautiful. There was another piece of Copenhagen china. There was a new nightdress and an amusing case to keep it in. There were very pretty boxes for her knick-knacks, some grand bedroom slippers and, at the very bottom of the parcel, something she had always wanted—a diamond wrist watch.

After the present opening it was time for tea and Christmas cake. Afterwards they roasted chestnuts and examined each other's Christmas presents and then there was music.

"Almost," said Lydia at last, "we've sung every carol."

"It is time we stopped," Alice agreed. "I must get supper if anybody can eat any more and then it's time for bed."

"Oh dear! " said Ann. "Bed! After this glorious day it feels as if nothing nice would ever happen again."

"There is my party and presentation," Philip reminded her.

"And," said Robin, "in March it do be my birthday. my dear soul."

CHAPTER TWENTY-THREE: THE PRESENTATION

THOUGH Ann had thought nothing nice was ever going to happen again something nice was to happen quite soon. For Philip and Alice had decided that on the presentation evening Alice would take the children to the pantomime.

Although pantomimes in many places were dying out Headstone was quite famous for its pantomimes. Always the theatre booked a star comedian for the dame and a well-known singer and dancer for the principal boy. This year the pantomime was "Cinderella".

Because they had booked early the family sat in the front row of the dress circle. Wonderful seats, not too near to spoil the full glory of the transformation scene and in a position where nobody could spoil their view.

"I bet everyone is envying us," Lydia whispered to Gemma, who was sitting next to her.

"They are gorgeous seats," Robin, who was on Gemma's other side, agreed, "but I wish I could be cut in half, sometimes here and sometimes at Dad's dinner. I do hope he makes a good speech."

"He will," said Alice. "Your father is a good after dinner speaker."

"But this is different," Ann reminded her. "It's a dinner for him with all the important people there, like the mayor."

"What I want to know," said Gemma, "is what are they going to give him?"

Alice had to whisper in case the people behind had subscribed to the present.

"As you know I'm terrified it will be a silver salver. Signed all over and dreadful to clean."

"I think you'll have to settle for it being silver," Ann whispered. "I think presentations usually are. I bet it's a cigarette box. They won't know Dad's given up smoking."

"I still think it might be a gold watch," said Lydia.

Soon what might be happening to Philip was forgotten because the orchestra played the overture and then the curtain rose on a room in the house where Cinderella lived.

Everything and everybody in the pantomime was admired by the children, but to Lydia the most interesting performers were a troupe of twenty-four children. This was because they had two numbers to themselves during which they tap danced.

"Watch it," she whispered to Gemma. "Though they are further on than you are it's the same steps. Listen while I count 8—and 1 2 and 3 and—4 and 5 6 and 7 and—"

Gemma listened, it certainly was the same counting as she had to do at her dancing class. It was pleasant to watch too and the audience loved it. She must work harder next term. Suppose the drama school gave a matinée to help raise the £10,000, wouldn't it be wonderful if she was good enough to dance! The troupe had no solo dancer so Gemma for once did not think of herself in a solo part.

The second time the troupe danced alone Lydia gave Gemma a furious nudge.

"Watch this carefully. It's the shuffle I'm always teaching you. Look, it goes forward and back like I tell you. Shuffle shuffle shuffle shuffle, hop step tap."

In the interval Alice bought them ices and they discussed the pantomime. Ann and Robin agreed that Cinderella had a lovely singing voice, they were not so sure about the Prince, for both Ann and Robin thought her voice forced, but they agreed she looked marvellous and sang quite well enough for Prince Charming.

129

E

"I'm so fascinated by those little children," said Alice. "They are only tots and they dance beautifully."

Lydia bounced on her seat.

"Especially tap. Oh, I wish I was them."

"Well you can't be," Alice said firmly. "Imagine what Miss Arrowhead would say."

Gemma, gazing at her relations, marvelled at their ignorance. How could people know so little!

"Those aren't tots, Aunt Alice. They have to be twelve or they wouldn't be allowed a licence."

"Twelve! I can't believe it," Alice protested. "They don't look more than seven or eight."

"I expect they pretended to be twelve," Ann suggested.

"You can't do that," Gemma explained. "When you apply for a licence you have to show your birth certificate."

"So even if Miss Arrowhead didn't mind," said Robin, "Lydie couldn't get a licence."

"Not for three Aprils," Ann pointed out. "She'll be ten next April, eleven the April after and then the next one she'll be twelve."

"Oh well," said Lydia, "it's a good thing I can't get a licence for Miss Arrowhead would be mad as a wasp if I did."

In the last act Buttons sang a song about roses in June. It had a catchy chorus so he asked each part of the house to sing it on their own to see which could sing the loudest. This was, of course, a challenge to the family.

"Even you have got to sing loud now," Robin whispered to Gemma.

When it came to the dress circle's turn no other part of the house had a chance for the family in the front row led the rest to victory.

Buttons, sheltering his eyes from the footlights, came to the front of the stage and looked up at the circle.

"It seemed to me," he said, "I heard some very nice singing up there. Would that family in the front row sing alone please."

Alice was embarrassed but the children were delighted. especially at the clapping which they got at the end.

But that was not the end of the excitement for, just as everybody on the stage all dressed in white were marching down the grand staircase at the end of the pantomime, one of the programme girls nudged Ann, who was sitting in the gang-way seat.

"It was you lot that sang alone, wasn't it?"

"Yes," said Ann.

The girl produced an enormous box of chocolates.

"This is for you with the compliments of the management."

After so much dazzle and laughter and success Trelawny Drive looked rather dreary when they got home.

"I wish everything was always pantomime," said Lydia

Alice knew just how she felt.

"It's chicken soup and jelly for supper. How would that seem to you with one of our chocolates to top it off?"

The children, full of supper, were in bed and nearly asleep by the time Philip came home, but they heard him and woke each other up to run to the top of the stairs.

"Did you make a good speech, Dad?"

"What did they give you, Dad? Was it a cigarette box?"

"Aunt Alice said it would be a silver salver. Was it?"

"I bet it was a gold watch. Wasn't it, Dad?"

"Did you have a lovely evening, Dad? We did and we won a box of chocolates. Cinderella had a gorgeous voice. Even you would say it was well trained."

Philip came to the bottom of the stairs.

"Put on your dressing-gowns and look out of the window."

There was a mad rush and scramble, then the windows were thrown open and the children were hanging out. There was a street light outside their gate and under it was standing the presentation. It was greeted by a scream.

"It's a car! A car! We've got a motor car!"

CHAPTER TWENTY-FOUR: NEWS FOR GEMMA

IT was gorgeous having a car and Philip was very generous using it. Before he married he had driven his mother's so he had kept up his driving licence, for often when The Steen was on tour he had driven from one town to another with a friend who had a car, and he had taken his share of driving. That holiday the car was especially needed for, apart from endless Christmas parties and concerts at which Ann sang, even by the beginning of the year Raise-ten-thousand-pounds fever had hit Headstone. There was seldom a day when there was not a coffee morning, a bring-and-buy sale or, worse still, a committee.

"If things are like this now," Alice groaned, "what will they be like by the middle of the year?"

"I just can't bear to think," said Ann. "Our church choir is joining with all the others for that choir festival, if all the singers who say they are coming to the concert come it ought to make most of the ten thousand by itself. And I hate to think how much rehearsing there will be with the school choir for the pageant music."

"It'll be worse for me," Robin pointed out. "We've not only got the choir festival but there's going to be our own concert of church music. The choir master says people are already buying tickets."

"Miss Lydie Robinson is going to be busy too," said Lydia. "The junior mixed are doing a maypole dance, and three other dances in the folk dancing concert and Miss Lydie Robinson is dancing in them all."

"My goodness!" thought Gemma listening to them. "I do hope Miss Jenkins finds me a part, however tiny, in the pageant or I'm going to be the only one of the family who is doing nothing."

Though Gemma did not know it the day after school reassembled there was a meeting of those teachers concerned in the pageant. Mr. Weldon had finished writing it during the Christmas holiday and was quite excited about it.

"As most of you know, last autumn as soon as I knew what was planned I went to London. There I studied the Open Air theatre in Regent's Park. I am thankful to say it is possible in our park to reproduce a very similar stage. Natural trees in the background and others round the stage and auditorium on which to hang loud speakers. In some ways we are more fortunate than Regent's Park because we have a slight natural slope up from the stage which forms a rake, so the audience should see perfectly."

"Does that mean," one of the teachers asked, "that we can have speaking parts as we would in a theatre?"

"Exactly." Mr. Weldon looked at Mr. Seddon for corroboration. "I'm afraid most of the speaking parts are for boys and, as you would suppose, Mr. Seddon has been forced to throw a fairly wide net to give us local history."

"I have indeed," Mr. Seddon agreed. "For instance, I've used the building of the monastery. Well, it was built thirty miles away. Mr. Weldon has written a good part for the Prior and two or three other monks have good parts."

"I have managed a part for a witch," said Mr. Weldon, "and there is a wife in the Black Death scene and Miss Hattie Boak appears—she was the first head of the Red Cloak School—but there's precious little else for the girls except as sort of glorified crowds."

"There is a girl as well as a boy who link the whole pageant together, isn't there?" Mr. Seddon asked.

133

Mr. Weldon nodded.

"Yes, two school children. They may have to come from outside the drama group because they must be small so that the other characters appear tall. I mean we can't have the highwaymen and the children all the same height."

"There is Sammy Birtwistle," one of the teachers suggested.

There was a groan from everybody. Sammy Birtwistle was the bane of the drama group. He was so small he was almost a dwarf. Though he was rising fifteen his voice had not broken and he spoke in a shrill nasal pipe. But because of his height he had been used in various plays where a boy was needed, and all who had produced him remembered only too vividly the heartbreak of teaching him to say his lines. To add to the trouble of teaching Sammy he had a Mum who thought he was a genius. It was she who had forced him on the drama group, and was round at the school making a scene if in each production a part was not found for "our Sammy".

"Oh dear, yes! I'm afraid it's a natural for Sammy." Mr. Weldon turned sympathetically to Miss Jenkins. "I'm afraid this looks like trouble for you because you did say you would undertake any coaching that was needed."

Miss Jenkins nodded in agreement but her mind was not on Sammy. She was thinking of Gemma.

"We have a little girl in the drama group. She joined last term. She is a very small eleven-year old. She is in 2.P."

Mr. Weldon looked doubtful.

"The two children have a good deal to say, they're on stage all the way through, do you think this child could cope?"

Miss Jenkins decided to keep Gemma to herself for the time being. It would be fun to surprise them all.

"I think she will be all right," was all she said.

Not knowing that there was a meeting of the producers

of the pageant, still less that Miss Jenkins was putting her forward for the most important girl's part, Gemma was feeling almost as out of things as she had when she first came to the house. It was the final blow when the day of the pageant meeting Lydia came dashing in to the sitting-room after a private lesson with Miss Arrowhead and called out:

"I'm dancing in your school pageant, Ann."

Ann was laying the table for tea.

"Are you? What as? I didn't know there was any dancing."

Lydia was always excited after a dancing class, now she pirouetted round the table as she talked.

"There are to be thousands of fairies. Green all over with green wings. We are hidden before the pageant starts. Then we come out and dance and make a fairy ring. Then we lead two children from your school and make them sit in the fairy ring. That's how they see the past, which is the pageant. There's no solos to dance but Miss Arrowhead says she'll want me to lead a group of dancers."

"I thought Miss Arrowhead wouldn't let you dance in public," said Gemma.

"Oh, she doesn't mind about this. It isn't proper dancing, just skipping about with bare feet. Miss Arrowhead says it'll be a counting thing—you know, doing things on a beat."

"Are you coming to the school for rehearsals?" Ann asked.

"No. Only in the park. Two ordinary rehearsals on the stage and the dress rehearsal."

"That's good," said Ann, "because honestly I don't see how you could find time. Come to that, I don't see how any of us could squeeze in any more."

"Except you, Gemma," Robin pointed out. "You aren't doing anything."

Ann knew Gemma would hate that.

"I expect she'll be awfully busy when the time comes.

135

All the drama group who aren't acting will be; imagine, with all the school taking part, the rushing around there'll be to see everybody is in the right place."

Gemma managed to hide it but inside she was appalled. She had not sat in the punishment chair to get Mr. Stevens to help her into the drama group to become a glorified call boy.

When Gemma was happy it seemed to shine out of her all over. When she was unhappy that came out of her, too, so that she seemed wrapped in a dark cloud. This dimmed her personality so that while the mood lasted she looked a very ordinary but rather sullen schoolgirl.

The next morning Gemma arrived at school in one of her black moods. Miss Jenkins had met Miss Pepper in the staff cloakroom that morning and had confided to her the plans she had for Gemma.

"I'm not saying anything about her to the producer until I see how she shapes. But really, if you had heard her recite! Such a golden child, I tell you, for those few minutes she was Titania."

Miss Pepper, waiting for the children to settle down before she gave them their first arithmetic problem, thought "Poor Miss Jenkins! She wouldn't think much of her golden child if she could see Gemma now." It crossed her mind to tell Gemma right away that Miss Jenkins wanted to see her after school, but she did not like scowling children so she decided to keep the news until the last minute.

When Gemma was told the change in her was dramatic. The cloud disappeared as if it had never been and she glowed all over.

"Oh, thank you, Miss Pepper! I do hope it means there's a part for me in the pageant."

Miss Jenkins was waiting for Gemma in the gymnasium where she took rehearsals.

"There you are, Gemma! You remember Mr. Seddon
136

on the first day of last term told us that the pageant would be linked together by a boy and a girl . . ."

Gemma jumped ahead of her. She stepped forward and for a moment Miss Jenkins thought she was going to hug her.

"Oh, darling Miss Jenkins! How gorgeous! I thought perhaps a little part but I never hoped for the girl because Mr. Seddon said she was on all through the pageant."

Enthusiasm of Gemma's sort was anathema to Miss Jenkins. Control, control and more control was her creed. Coldly she held up one hand.

"You are preceding me. I was going to say I was prepared to try you as the girl. You may not prove suitable."

But Gemma was at that moment uncrushable.

"Oh, but I will be suitable. So suitable I couldn't be more suitabler. Dear Miss Jenkins, you'll never, never know how happy you've made me."

When Gemma left the room Miss Jenkins looked after her with a worried frown. What had she taken on? Titania was one thing and so was reciting but this was a modern part. "Dear me!" she thought. "Let's hope the child is good because I can foresee a lot of trouble getting rid of her if she isn't."

CHAPTER TWENTY-FIVE: REHEARSAL

JUNE had sounded such a long way off when the pageant was first talked about, but now suddenly it seemed to be happening almost at once. Nor was the pageant all, some of the money-raising events were already taking place. The choir festival was over. It had been a tremendous success and had not only raised money but had brought a lot of musical people to Headstone, and this had meant there were reports on the concerts in the national press. This was splendid from Headstone's point of view but not so lucky for the Robinsons.

"Philip," Alice said one morning, looking up from a letter she was reading, "I am devoted to your mother but I can't feel June is a good month for her to stay with us."

Philip looked surprised.

"I should have thought it was a very good month. She can see the pageant, that will mean she will hear Ann sing and watch Lydie dance, she'll love it."

"She won't hear me sing," said Ann. "I mean except with the choir."

"And I wouldn't call what I do dancing," Lydia pointed out.

"Why don't you ask her in October when you have your concert?" Robin suggested. "Then quite likely we'll all be doing something."

"Don't remind me of that awful concert," Alice pleaded. "I thought at first it was a mercy it was not until the autumn as it gave me more time. But what is going to happen is that everybody with any talent has exhausted

138

themselves earlier in the year. Except for a miracle you children will be all the concert there is."

"Well, Gran would love that," said Robin.

Ann saw the difficulties.

"But the audience wouldn't. In fact, if it was only us, I bet they wouldn't pay to come in."

"No, I suppose it will have to be June," Alice admitted. "Gran always has chosen her own date."

"And she can see Gemma," Lydia pointed out. "After all, she's got the biggest part in the pageant."

"That's not going to interest your grandmother," said Gemma. "I'm no relation to her."

Alice smiled.

"She's a very outspoken person so you'll have to do well, Gemma, or she'll say you shouldn't call yourself Robinson."

Because all the speaking parts were being acted by the drama group the school only heard rumours about what was going on. But since the leading characters spoke to the two children Ann had heard in a roundabout way that Gemma was considered very good.

"They say you're marvellous," she told Gemma with pride. "But I suppose you would be, it's easy for you."

"If Gran thinks you're good," said Robin, "she'll say pride comes before a fall."

Actually, now that Gemma had got what she wanted, she was not in the least conceited. She might easily have been because the drama group and all the producers thought she was outstanding. She had a long part for after the first rehearsals lines that should have been said by Sammy Birtwistle were taken away and given to her. In fact Sammy's part by degrees was cut to the bone until he had only the minimum to say in each scene. Luckily he was too dense to notice and his Mum was not at rehearsals to notice for him.

The children were the linchpins which held the pageant together. They were supposed to be two children from the

Comprehensive school who, through fairy magic, saw things that had happened in the past more or less where the school now stood. In each scene the principal actor told the children what they were doing or going to do and something about themselves. In the case of a group on pilgrimage to Canterbury it was all talk until the procession rode away. But in scenes such as the highwayman scene, though the children talked to the highwayman they moved to the side of the stage and watched the scene where a coach was held up and the passengers robbed.

Gemma was so busy and so happy she was not even excited about her birthday though she did enjoy the film they went to see as a celebration. But even while the film lasted she kept remembering the pageant, the glorious pageant that was already making Gemma Robinson into a person and not a nondescript child in 2.P.

In May it was decided there would be a general rehearsal for the whole school to give an idea where their class scenes fitted in. Because there were no loudspeakers outside it was planned this would be held in the assembly hall. This was large enough to hold a near replica of the park stage, it was marked out on the floor with tapes, and the trees were represented by chairs. It could only be a rough rehearsal because for one thing there could be no horses. Many children from the school had riding lessons on Saturdays so horses, as in the Canterbury and highwayman scenes, were much used in the pageant. But all the producers wanted was a rough idea of how the finished pageant would look.

There was a big gallery at the back of the assembly hall, and there was the stage and there were seats round the walls, and into these spaces squashed all the school not concerned in a scene. To begin with there was a lot of whispering and giggling and some of the boys galloped round to represent the absent horses. But there was silence when the choir began to sing. This was the fairy music during which Lydia and a hundred children from

140

different dancing schools would be dancing. At the end of the dance they were to pull Gemma and Sammy, who could not see them, into their fairy ring. The children then had to look up at the sky.

"What was that music?" Sammy squeaked.

Gemma raised one arm and pointed above her head.

"It must have been a lark but I never heard a lark sing like that before."

It had been hoped that Sammy would get a laugh on his reply.

"Some lark!" But as Sammy said it the line dropped like a stone. At once Gemma picked the scene up.

"It could have been a lark. Remember what Shelley wrote:

> 'Higher still and higher
>   From the earth thou springest,
> Like a cloud of fire;
>   The blue deep thou wingest,
> And singing still dost soar, and soaring ever singest.'"

"Look!" Sammy said. "Look!"

What he was looking at was the entrance of pilgrims on the road to Canterbury.

By now the school were nudging each other, mostly asking "Who's she?" But form 2P glowed, a performance like Gemma's would surely earn House marks.

From her place in the chorus Ann swelled with pride. "Yes, she's my cousin," she whispered over and over again, and in reply got "Isn't she pretty!" "Doesn't she speak nicely!" "She's ever so good, your cousin."

The result of that rehearsal was more than Gemma had dreamed it could be. She was known by sight by all the school and even talked to by some very high up pupils, and the head of Jane Austen House came specially from her exalted top classroom to speak to her.

"We've had a special house meeting. If you give a performance like you gave at rehearsal when we act the pageant you will win five points for your House."

Gemma did not care if she won a hundred points, but it was lovely being known as belonging to Jane Austen.

"Thank you so much," she said. "I promise I'll try."

Another advantage of everybody having seen the pageant rehearsal was that she was fussed over. "Have you a rehearsal today, Gemma?" the music mistress would ask and if Gemma said yes—and by that time there was a rehearsal every day—she was told not to join in the song but to sit down and rest. The games' mistress treated her as if she was made of glass. "I don't think you better do any gym until after the pageant, dear. I shall never hear the last of it if somebody bumps your nose." Even Miss Pepper took special care of her. "You need not do this homework, Gemma. I know you have a rehearsal every evening and you should get to bed early."

Only at home was there no fuss. Alice was too used to performers to pay particular attention to one. She did say:

"Ann tells me you are going to be good in the pageant, darling. I'm so proud," but in the next breath she added: "It's your table laying day, isn't it? Everything's ready, it's hot plates."

Gemma didn't mind lack of praise at home. She had long ago accepted her cousins' various talents. But it was heaven to be using her own again and so to be equal to them.

Then, early in June, Philip's mother arrived to stay and this faced Gemma with a totally unexpected complication.

142

CHAPTER TWENTY-SIX: DRESS REHEARSAL

GRAN looked a fat cosy sort of person. Sometimes this was true for she was in her sixties and set in her ways, but there was another side to her. She was proud of all her children but she had been proud to bursting point of Philip. Amongst her friends it was accepted that somehow on every occasion she would bring in "My son Philip who plays the violin with The Steen." It had been a terrible blow to her when Philip had written to tell her he had resigned from The Steen and was going to teach. She had kept her grief to herself saying "never rub salt into a wound," but keeping silent had not really helped, it had only driven the pain inside her.

There was, however, one ray of comfort in Philip's letter and this she had clung to and built on to. It came at the end of the letter.

"There is a bright side to my having to resign. I shall be able to undertake the early training of Ann's voice myself, it's early days yet but it looks as if she is going to have an outstanding singing voice. Miss Arrowhead, who teaches Lydie, believes she has the makings of a real dancer. And the head of St. Giles' choir school is getting steamed up about Robin, he believes he is shaping up to be a future solo boy. I don't know what I've done to have such promising children."

So it was as the proud grandmother of brilliant children that Gran descended on Headstone. It was going to be a lovely visit she was sure during which she would move from entertainment to entertainment, at most of which one grandchild at least would perform and she could glow with reflected glory.

Philip took time off to meet his mother with the car and the old lady was delighted.

"It's a beautiful car. But no more than you deserve, Philip dear, after all you did for The Steen, and it's beautifully kept."

"It's the pride of the family," Philip explained. "All the children help clean it."

Gran nodded.

"Many hands make light work. Now tell me about the children. When am I hearing and seeing them perform?"

"If you are not too tired you can hear Robin tonight, or rather watch him for, of course, you can't pick out his voice. St. Giles are giving three performances of church music. This is the last night, it's been a real treat."

"Isn't he singing a solo?"

Philip laughed.

"Give him a chance. He only became a chorister at Christmas."

"What about this pageant? I understand Lydie is dancing in it."

Philip was busy steering the car through difficult traffic so he had only half an ear for his mother.

"That's right."

"Splendid! I have never seen her dance. And dear Ann is singing."

"That's right."

"When is it?"

Philip had steered clear of the traffic block.

"The pageant? All next week but there is a dress rehearsal on Saturday so, as we have to collect the children, Alice thought you might like to come and watch. Like all dress rehearsals it is sure to be a terrible muddle but it will be all the more pleasing when we see the proper performance."

It had been arranged that Philip would go back to the

music school after delievering Gran so the children would look after her until Alice got back from the hospital. Happy with the arrangements Gran unpacked and came down to the sitting-room for tea. There were, she saw, four children in the room. She had been told about Alice's niece, Gemma, but it had slipped her mind. "How lucky," she thought, "instead of individual presents I brought a family present of a big box of chocolates."

"Oh Gran!" said Ann, throwing her arms round her. "I'm so glad you've come."

"So am I," Robin shouted, hugging her from the back.

"And so am I," said Lydia. "And Miss Lydie Robinson would like to kiss you when there's room."

Gran smiled.

"It's the early bird catches the worm, you know, Lydie."

"Oh Gran, this is Gemma," said Ann.

Gran gave Gemma a kind look.

"I know, you're my daughter-in-law's niece. Gemma Alston."

Gran was now sitting so Lydia put an arm round her neck.

"No, Gran. It's Aunt Rowena who is Alston. Gemma is . . ."

Ann hurriedly interrupted.

"She's Robinson while she's staying with us. Mum thought it was easier."

"One set of marking tapes for all of us," Robin explained.

Ann went to get the tea and while she was gone, though she talked to Lydia and Robin, Gran was studying Gemma. "They can call her Robinson if they like," she thought, "but she is not a bit like my family, she's an Alston through and through."

Gran enjoyed the church music at St. Giles though she complained in a loud whisper when the solo boys sang

145

that Robin would have done better. By the Saturday she had settled into her usual niche in the family and was looking forward to the evening's dress rehearsal.

"Never mind how many mistakes there are," she told the girls. "If at first you don't succeed try, try, try again."

Somehow it had passed unnoticed by everybody that she had not been told what part Gemma played in the pageant. This was partly because they had as a family come to take Gemma's leading part for granted, but largely it was because nobody thought Gran would be particularly interested, it was a family joke that in her opinion nobody did anything well except her kith and kin.

All dress rehearsals are apt to be a muddle. The hundred fairies supposed to be hidden behind trees and in the grass were all in the wrong places, and most of them in the wrong positions with their tails stuck up in the air. A worried huddle of dancing teachers came on to the stage and sorted the children out. But the fairy music had to be sung three times before the pageant started. Then it was Gemma who took command. Others might falter and forget their lines but not her. She had not been a professional since she was a small child for nothing. Firmly gripping Sammy—who showed signs of running away—by the wrist she cut his first line, which he was clearly never going to say, and raising her arm to the sky she said: "That music must have been a lark, but I never heard a lark sing like that before." She gave Sammy's arm a pinch so that in a bleat he cried out "Some lark!" and for the first and last time got his laugh.

In spite of all the muddles and the going back to do a scene again, Philip, Alice and Robin enjoyed themselves. It was a lovely evening, the air scented with roses, and in spite of everything it was clear the pageant would be a fine, colourful affair. Then, of course, there was Gemma. They had expected her to be good but she was so much more, there was something about her which made you have to look at her whoever else was on the stage.

146

When the interval came Philip turned smiling to his mother.

"Allowing for a few sticky patches I thought that was a pretty fine effort, didn't you?"

Gran got up.

"I did not. I thought it was ruined by that girl."

"What girl?" Alice asked.

"Your niece Gemma. Posturing, affected child. I don't want to see any more of it. I'm going home."

Philip drove his mother home and then came back and joined Alice and Robin.

"Look, old man," he said to Robin, "I've got to have your word you won't repeat anything Gran said to the girls. We can't have poor Gemma upset before the pageant starts."

Robin dismissed that.

"Don't fuss. I wasn't going to say anything. Gran was only cross because it's Gemma who is important and not Ann and Lydie. Any fool can see Gemma's fabulous."

As soon as all the family got home Alice, having given the children supper, sent them up to bed. Then she and Philip discussed things over a cup of tea.

"I forgot what a family woman my mother was," said Philip. "What are we going to do? You know what her tongue's like. She's sure to tell Gemma what she pretends she thinks of her."

Alice had decided what to do.

"Leave it to me. I'll have a talk with Gemma and warn her to look out for squalls."

"I wish for her sake Gemma hadn't taken on this part," said Philip. "She stands out so. I should think someone is sure to spot her and that is the last thing she wants. We must be careful my mother doesn't remember who she is."

Alice nodded.

"I'll warn the child. But, bless her! Wasn't she good? Everybody was talking about her. I don't think, however

147

hurtful Gran is, that it will affect her much. She must know what a success she is."

The next morning Alice kept Gemma in bed for breakfast and the moment Ann had gone to church she came up to see her. She sat on the bed.

"You were wonderful, darling, but I'm afraid you've made an enemy. Old Gran is furious you are the star and not her grandchildren. She's always been like that."

Gemma knew she was good, and that the producers and the school thought she was good, so she could not really care what one old lady thought.

"I'm sorry. But what can I do?"

"Nothing. Only don't answer back. She'll quote proverbs to you. But I don't want you getting on the wrong side of her. She has at the moment forgotten, if she ever knew, that your surname is Bow. She thinks you are an Alston like I was and your mother is. But if she remembers I am afraid she will tell everybody, for I think to hear that you are a professional actress would make you being so good easier to bear."

Gemma gazed at Alice in horror. It was not only old Gran who would be interested to know who she was. She had never wanted the school to know but now, if they knew it, all her glory would be gone, everybody would say "Oh well, it's easy for her, she's a professional."

"Oh, she mustn't know! Please tell the others not to tell her."

"I will. And when you come down never mind how rude the old lady is, keep your temper and answer politely."

It was lucky Alice had talked to Gemma so that she was prepared, for when she came downstairs dressed for church Gran said in a very meaning way:

"Look who's here! But it's not the hen who cackles most that lays the largest egg."

To which Gemma replied with a polite smile:

"Good morning, Mrs. Robinson."

CHAPTER TWENTY-SEVEN: AN IDEA IS BORN

EVERYBODY had prophesied it would rain all through the pageant week. But everybody was wrong. It was the finest week in June anybody could remember. As a result every seat was sold and coach loads of people, hearing how good the pageant was, streamed into Headstone.

"I shouldn't think there's ever been so many people here before," said Robin. "Headstone is famous."

Fortunately it was quite easy to keep Gemma and Gran apart. For she and Ann had left for school before she was up in the morning. Both girls stayed at school all day and then were marched with their class, with Miss Pepper in charge, to the park. There a catering firm provided tea and cakes and cold drinks, and then it was time for everybody to change for the pageant began at six o'clock.

Gemma had no real changing to do because she had to wear her school uniform, but she kept a clean frock in the tent where she dressed, and then went to Miss Jenkins who gave her a slight make-up and brushed out her hair, for it had been decided she might wear it loose for the pageant. After the performance Philip picked the girls up in the car and directly they got in they were sent up to bed where they ate their supper off trays. So whatever Gran might have saved up to say she never got a chance.

"You wait for Sunday," said Ann, "when the pageant's over, that'll be Gran's moment."

Gemma hated to think of Sunday, not because of Gran, the old lady could say what she liked, but because the pageant would be finished. By Monday she would be just

Gemma Robinson again, one of the girls in 2.P. It would be awful.

On the last night of the pageant Gran—making a great favour of it—agreed to watch the performance.

"After all," she said, "you have bought a seat for me and I hate to see money wasted. Save the pennies and the pounds will look after themselves."

Everybody in the town who could came to that last performance. The mayor and mayoress were there, he wearing his chain of office. The Steen were not playing that week-end so all the orchestra seemed to have turned up. Philip was constantly waving to old friends. Robin's choirmaster and a large number of the boys from St. Giles were there. And two rows in front of the Robinsons sat Miss Arrowhead and Polly.

In the interval Philip went off to talk to his friends and so did Robin, but not so much to talk as to hear the boys hint that they would like to meet Gemma. Miss Arrowhead and Polly, seeing there were two empty seats beside Alice, asked if they could sit in them for a few minutes. Alice introduced Gran. Long experience as a dancing teacher had taught Miss Arrowhead that praising other people's children seldom went down well, and she had not forgotten that in spite of being called Robinson Gemma belonged to Alice's side of the family, so she talked about Lydia.

"You are going to be very proud of her one day," she told Gran. "If she goes on improving as she is now she could make a very talented dancer."

Gran almost squirmed she was so pleased.

"And she's not the only one," she said in a don't-dare-deny-it tone. "Ann has a lovely singing voice."

"And the little boy is in the choir school, isn't he?" Polly asked.

Alice nodded.

"He is and doing well. I'm awfully glad to have a chance to talk to you, Miss Arrowhead. In October I am on the

150

organising committee for a concert to be run by the hospital. It's the last event in the Raise-ten-thousand-pounds year. It sounded all right in the spring when we were planning it, but it looks very different now. Every bit of talent for miles around has been used already. I suppose you can't recommend any one?"

Miss Arrowhead thought about that.

"I'm afraid not. I'm against my pupils dancing in public, it means taking them off their regular routine to fix in rehearsals."

Alice sighed, she had been expecting that answer but it was disappointing.

"Ann is going to sing, I had hoped with either the school choir or the church choir, but they both say there can be no more concerts this year so she will sing alone. Bless her, she will sing beautifully as she always does, but unfortunately people are used to hearing her. I shall get Robin to sing, too, but he'll be busy by then, the school choir start early preparing for Christmas."

"What about professionals?" Miss Arrowhead suggested. "A TV personality is always a draw."

"I don't know any," Alice confessed. "Nor do any of the committee."

"What about Gemma?" Polly asked. "Couldn't she do something? She's a most accomplished little actress."

"I think the town has seen enough of Gemma," said Gran. "If she appears in Alice's concert they may say it never rains but it pours."

Miss Arrowhead got up.

"We must get back to our seats." She shook Gran's hand and smiled good-bye at Alice. "You should try and think of some way of putting your clever family on the stage as a group. That might be a draw."

The pageant was over. The mayor had come on to the stage at the end and congratulated everybody, especially Mr. Weldon for writing the pageant, and all who had worked to produce it. He was proud to announce that in spite of heavy expenses the pageant had made a thousand pounds. Then everybody sang "God Save the Queen" and it was all over.

In bed that night Gemma, as soon as Ann was asleep, cried and cried. It seemed unbearable that she would come down tomorrow to any ordinary day, and that on Monday there would be school and homework and dull 2.P. just as if nothing had happened.

No amount of planning could prevent Gran and Gemma meeting on Sunday but Gran, to everyone's surprise, though she did not say much to Gemma, was quite pleasant. The truth was she was a perspicacious old lady and she could see there was no need for anyone to remind Gemma that her glory had departed. She was in one of her dark moods when every bit of colour was drained from her. Listlessly she ate her breakfast. Listlessly she went to her room to make her bed and listlessly came down dressed for church. "No need to tell you pride comes before a fall," Gran thought. "You know you are Miss Nobody this morning."

That afternoon Philip and Alice were going to tea with friends and Lydia and Robin were also invited. Ann had to go to church as she was singing at a children's service so Gran and Gemma were alone in the house.

"You must be tired, darling," Alice said to Gemma before she left. "Why don't you take a deck chair in the garden?"

"All right," Gemma agreed as she would have agreed to anything that day. So presently she took a deck chair to the bottom of the garden and settled down to re-read "The Secret Garden". But it was hot and she was almost asleep when she heard scrunch, scrunch on the gravel path and there was Gran carrying another deck chair. Gran was the last person Gemma wanted to see but she jumped up and helped open the chair and placed it beside her own.

"I'm glad to have this chance to talk to you," Gran said.

"I have been thinking about you. You are Gemma Bow, aren't you?"

Gemma's heart dropped like a stone. So who she was had to come out after all.

"Yes, but I don't want anyone to know. That's why Aunt Alice suggested I should call myself Robinson."

"Oh, what a fearful web we weave when once we practise to deceive," said Gran. "But you being Gemma Bow could have its uses. You are accustomed to making a show of yourself on the stage, anyone can see that."

"Well, more in pictures," Gemma explained.

"It comes to the same thing. What I have been thinking is this. Do you think you could turn my grandchildren into a group for my daughter-in-law's concert? I should imagine Miss Arrowhead would allow Lydie to dance if it was in a family group. They will be more noticeable than each of them coming on by themselves. It will draw attention to them as a family."

Gemma knew just what Gran meant. Earlier in the year after one of Ann's concerts she had tried tactfully to persuade her to make more of herself on the stage. For though she came on and sang beautifully, the moment her song was over she rushed off as if she had done something of which she was ashamed.

"If you mean the way I come on and off the stage," Ann had said, "I know it's awful. But I can't do it better so don't tell me about it because it fusses me."

But as part of a group Ann would probably feel quite different, she would have the rest of the family to keep her company.

"Do you mean just the cousins or me, too?"

"Well, I've been thinking about that. Can you do anything?"

Gemma answered from her heart.

"Nothing like they can. I've only a small voice but I can sing a bit to a banjo and I do a little tap dancing."

Gran looked at Gemma with approval.

"We can't all have the same gifts. But I reckon with your training you are the one to get this group going Think about it."

So Gemma thought and as she thought the cloud of depression lifted from her. She could not see exactly what they would all do but she could imagine herself and Ann and Lydie all dressed alike. That evening she called Lydia to join her and Ann in their bedroom.

"Your Gran talked to me about being a family group You know, a sort of sister act. We could all do our own things and some together. She thinks Miss Arrowhead might let you dance in a family group."

Lydia danced round the room.

"And tap dancing. Oh, I would love to do that! "

"We might call ourselves the Robinson sisters," Gemma suggested.

But Ann wouldn't hear of that.

"We couldn't. I mean you aren't a Robinson, think how we'd look if anyone found out because it's a sort of lie."

"Then what?" Gemma asked.

It was Lydia who had the idea.

"Gemma and Sisters. Oh, do let's be Gemma and Sisters! "

CHAPTER TWENTY-EIGHT: GEMMA AND SISTERS

It was the day of the hospital concert. Ann, Gemma and Lydia, all desperately nervous, were deposited by Philip at the stage entrance to the concert hall.

"Good luck, chicks. I'll see you on the stage," for Philip was sharing the accompaniments with Robin.

The girls' dresses were hung in their dressing-room. They were made of black plastic with white collars, with them they wore black tights. Lydia had wanted them to wear top hats like the tap dancers she had seen at the matinée, but she had been over-ruled because Ann would look odd singing a serious song in a top hat. So instead, round their heads, they wore wide black velvet bands.

Robin had firmly refused to be part of the group. It was, he said, a girls' thing, but he had agreed to come on in his ordinary clothes and play the accompaniment for the song he had swirled.

The girls were to finish the first half of the entertainment. Awed they looked at the programme. There it was— "Gemma and Sisters".

"It looks very important," said Lydia. "You know, as if we were quite famous."

"Oh dear, don't talk like that," Ann groaned. "Not before we appear for the very first time."

Gemma looked up and down the programme.

"Well, at least we're original. There's nothing else in the least like us."

155

The minutes ticked by and then at last they heard the bass who came before them singing "Old Man River".

"Come on," said Gemma. "And don't forget you're doing just what you ordinarily do only as a sister act."

It had not been a very interesting programme so far so the audience were delighted when the three girls, looking charming, ran on in their snappy outfits. Gemma knew that speed was important in their sort of turn. There must be no pauses or looking at each other. Straight away they put their heads together and sang Robin's swirled version of "O dear, what can the matter be?" which Robin thumped out on the piano. Then Philip slipped into the piano seat and Ann sang alone. Her voice was always lovely but that night it seemed to soar like a bird. Then Philip played the catchy music for Gemma and Lydia's tap dance. Then it was Gemma's turn. She picked her banjo off the top of the piano and softly sang "There was a lady loved a swine". Then Lydia danced her Irish jig.

The audience were quite hysterical. Who were these brilliant children? They were all so clever—the little dancer, the girl with the lovely voice and the one who played the banjo. As the curtain swung down there was a roar of applause.

Gran had arrived for the concert. She gave Alice a nudge.

"What did I tell you? When you were worrying away about this concert didn't I tell you it would be all right? You should mark my words—never trouble trouble till trouble troubles you."

But Alice, blinded with tears of pride, did not answer, instead she stumbled through the artists' entrance to hug her family.

They were not alone. A thin young man was with them.

"Oh darlings!" Alice gasped. "You were splendid!"

"Just what I was saying," said the young man. "I'm a theatrical agent so I ought to know. I handle some of the top groups. Work at it, girls, and I'll be watching you,

156

and come along to see you when this little lady"—he patted Lydia's head—"is old enough to have a licence."

"Goodness!" said Gemma when the young man had gone. "He's very important. I've heard about him."

Lydia pirouetted round the room.

"Imagine us being famous! "

"This is an exciting year," said Gemma. "How I wish we could see into the future so we knew what happens to us next."

Alice smiled proudly.

"Whatever happens next I am certain Gemma and Sisters will be part of it."

Thursday's Child

Noel Streatfeild

'Noel Streatfeild's position in the children's book world is unique. She has had all the accolades: a Carnegie Medal, a Bodley Head Monograph—and both critical and popular esteem . . . She is endlessly inventive, full of verve and real understanding of the surfaces of childhood.'

Times Literary Supplement

'The past comes to life with humour and grace in *Thursday's Child*, a period piece set at the turn of the century. Margaret Thursday makes a splendid heroine . . . A whole way of life springs brilliantly to life.' *Growing Point*

'Authenticity blends beautifully with romance . . . Children will love it.' *Daily Telegraph*

Thursday's Child 'promises to be a minor classic and it is enchantingly and appropriately illustrated by Peggy Fortnum.'

Birmingham Post

When Hitler Stole Pink Rabbit

JUDITH KERR

Anna was only nine in 1933, too busy with her school work and her friends to take much notice of the posters of Adolf Hitler and the menacing swastikas plastered over Berlin. Being Jewish, she thought, was just something you were because your parents and grandparents were Jewish. Suddenly Anna's father was unaccountably and frighteningly missing. Shortly after, she and her brother were hurried out of Germany by their mother with alarming secrecy. Then began their rootless, wandering existence as refugees. Their life was often difficult and sad, but Anna soon discovered that all that really mattered was that the family was together.

An outstanding book for readers of ten upwards.

The Warden's Niece

GILLIAN AVERY

Maria hated school. She couldn't do her lessons and the threat of having to wear a label marked 'slut' for blotchy work was the last straw. So, on the 18th May 1875, she decided to run away. And as her secret ambition was to be a professor at Oxford, it was not unnatural for her to escape to her uncle, the Warden of Canterbury College.

That was the beginning of a wildly adventurous summer with the three Smith brothers, aided and abetted by their splendidly eccentric tutor. But it was a summer when the Warden's niece proved to herself, the dusty scholars and the boys – who would grudgingly admit that she was slightly better than most girls – that she too could carry out a proper piece of research, gather together the clues and solve a mystery quite by herself.

A Likely Lad and *The Greatest Gresham* are also Lions.

Gillian Avery's books are for ten-year-olds and upwards.